HOUGHTON MIFFLIN COMPANY

BOSTON

NEW YORK

ATHENEUM PUBLISHERS

THE PLAY

THE BALLAD OF THE SAD CAFE

CARSON
MC CULLERS'
NOVELLA
ADAPTED TO
THE STAGE BY
EDWARD
ALBEE

This adaptation to the stage
of THE BALLAD OF THE SAD CAFE
is dedicated to Carson McCullers,
of course, with great love.

EDWARD ALBEE

FIRST PERFORMANCE

October 30, 1963, New York City, Martin Beck Theatre

THE NARRATOR	ROSCOE LEE BROWNE
RAINEY 1	LOUIS W. WALDON
RAINEY 2	DEANE SELMIER
STUMPY MAC PHAIL	JOHN C. BECHER
HENRY MACY	WILLIAM PRINCE
MISS AMELIA EVANS	COLLEEN DEWHURST
COUSIN LYMON	MICHAEL DUNN
EMMA HALE	ENID MARKEY
MRS. PETERSON	JENNY EGAN
MERLIE RYAN	ROBERTS BLOSSOM
HORACE WELLS	WILLIAM DUELL
HENRY FORD CRIMP	DAVID CLARKE
ROSSER CLINE	GRIFF EVANS
LUCY WILLINS	NELL HARRISON
MRS. HASTY MALONE	BETTE HENRITZE
MARVIN MACY	LOU ANTONIO
HENRIETTA FORD CRIMP, JR.	SUSAN DUNFEE
TOWNSPEOPLE	ERNEST AUSTIN
	ALICE DRUMMOND
	JACK KEHOE

Directed by ALAN SCHNEIDER

Set by BEN EDWARDS
Lighting by JEAN ROSENTHAL
Music by WILLIAM FLANAGAN
Production Stage Manager, JOHN MAXTONE-GRAHAM

THE BALLAD
OF THE
SAD CAFE

THE SET

One set: MISS AMELIA's *house (later the cafe) taking most of the stage, not centered, though, but tending to stage-right, leaving a playing area, stage-left, for the battle, which will take place out-of-doors.* MISS AMELIA's *house must be practical, in the sense that its interior will be used, both upstairs and down, and, as well, we must be able to see its exterior without entering it. The main street of the town runs before the porch of the house, parallel to the apron of the stage.*

THE BALLAD OF THE SAD CAFE

is meant to be played without an intermission

Noon sun; street deserted; house boarded up;
nothing moves, no one is to be seen; heat; quiet.
Music: under all or some of the following.

THE NARRATOR

The Ballad of the Sad Cafe. The Beginning.

This building here—this boarded-up house—is twice distinguished; it is the oldest building in town . . . and the largest. Of course, the town is not very old—nor is it very large. There isn't much to it, except the cotton mill, the two-room houses where the workers live, a few peach trees, a church with two water-colored windows, and a miserable main street only a hundred yards long. The town is lonesome—sad—like a place that is far off and estranged from all other places in the world. The winters here are short and raw . . . the summers—white with glare, and fiery hot. If you walk along the main street on an August afternoon, there is nothing whatever to do. *(Pause)* There is heat . . . and silence. *(Pause)* Notice that window up there; notice that second-story window; notice that shuttered window. There's someone living up there. *(Short pause)* These August afternoons there is absolutely nothing to do; you might as well walk down to the Fork Falls Road and watch the chain gang . . . listen to the men sing. Though . . .

> *(Here, the upstairs window mentioned before, slowly*
> *opens, and* MISS AMELIA'S *appearance at the window*
> *is described as it occurs)*

. . . look now; watch the window. *(Pause)* Sometimes, in the late afternoon, when the heat is at its worst, a hand will slowly open the shutter there, and a face will look down at the town . . . a terrible, dim face . . . like the faces known in dreams. The face will linger at the window for an hour or so,

> *(Silence for a moment or two, then, as the shutters*
> *are slowly closed)*

. . . then the shutters will be closed once more, and as likely as not there will not be another soul to be seen along the main street.

> *(Silence; a lighting change begins)*

But once . . . once, this building—this boarded-up house— was a cafe. Oh, there were tables with paper napkins, colored streamers hanging from the lamps, and great gatherings on Saturday nights.

> *(Perhaps an echo of such sounds here)*

It was the center of the town! And this cafe . . . this cafe was run by a Miss Amelia Evans . . . who lives up there even now . . . whose face, in the late afternoons, sometimes, when the heat is at its worst, can be seen peering out from that shuttered window.

> *(Now we are shifting to an April evening, eight years*
> *previous. The boarded-up house will become a gen-*
> *eral store, its interior and exterior both visible)*

We are going back in time now, back even before the opening of the cafe, for there are two stories to be told: How the cafe came into being . . . for there was not always a cafe . . . and how the cafe . . . died. How we came to . . . silence.

> *(By now it is night; the lights are dim in the general*
> *store, the interior of which is visible. During the fol-*
> *lowing paragraph, three townsmen saunter onstage,*
> *move to the porch in front of the store; two sit on*
> *the steps, one leans against a porch post or the build-*
> *ing itself)*

It is toward midnight; April . . . eight years ago. Most people are in bed, but several men of the town, for reasons we shall see directly, prefer the front steps of Miss Amelia's general store. It is the kind of night when it is good to hear from far away, across the dark fields, the slow song of a field hand on his way to make love; or when it is pleasant to sit quietly and pick a guitar, or simply to rest alone, and think of nothing at all. Talk . . . or stay silent.

(The focus of the scene is now on the general store. Brief tableau, held chord under it)

The men are STUMPY MACPHAIL, *and the* RAINEY TWINS, RAINEY 1 *and* RAINEY 2. THEY *are silent; then a figure is seen coming in the shadows from stage-right.*

MACPHAIL

Who is that? *(The figure continues advancing)* I said, who is that there?

RAINEY 1 *(A high, giggly voice)*

Why, it's Henry Macy; that's who it is.

RAINEY 2 *(HE, too)*

Henry Macy; Henry Macy.

MACPHAIL

Henry?

HENRY MACY
(In view now, by the porch. Nods)

Stumpy; evening. *(Then, to the twins)* Boys?

RAINEY 2

How you, Henry? And how is Marvin, Henry? How is your brother?

(RAINEY 1 *giggles*)

MACPHAIL

Now, now.

RAINEY 1

How is he enjoying his stay, Henry? How is he enjoying the penitentiary?

MACPHAIL

Quiet, you!

HENRY MACY (*Placating*)

Now, Stumpy . . .

MACPHAIL

You got no sense at all? You *all* foolish in the head? Talk about Marvin Macy, Miss Amelia nearby, maybe, God knows?
(RAINEY 2 *giggles*)
Miss Amelia hear that name, she knock you clear to Society City.

(*Both* RAINEYS *giggle*)

HENRY MACY (*A weary sigh*)

That true, Lord knows.

MACPHAIL

Knock you clear to Society City.

RAINEY 2

Miss Amelia ain't back. She at the still.

MACPHAIL

It don't matter.

RAINEY 1

You here for liquor, Henry?

HENRY MACY *(Distant)*

I just come by; just . . . by.

RAINEY 2

You not waiting on liquor, Henry?

MACPHAIL

He said he come by.

HENRY MACY *(To* MACPHAIL*)*

Miss Amelia digging up a barrel?

RAINEY 2 *(Giggling)*

He just come by.

HENRY MACY

I thirst for good liquor like any man; I thirst for Miss Amelia's liquor.

RAINEY 1 *(To* RAINEY 2*)*

We all waiting on liquor
(RAINEY 2 *giggles.*
A door in the rear of the general store opens; MISS AMELIA *enters, carrying several dark glass bottles.* SHE *is dressed in Levis and a cotton work shirt (red?), boots.* SHE *kicks the door shut with a foot. The sound is heard)*

MACPHAIL

Hm?

RAINEY 1

It Miss Amelia; it Miss Amelia back.

HENRY MACY (*Rising*)

That so?

RAINEY 2

Why, sure, less we got prowlers . . . thieves, people break-
ing in t'houses like some people . . .
  (*Both* RAINEYS *go into smothered giggles.* MISS
  AMELIA *carries the bottles to the store counter,
  puts them down, comes out onto the porch*)

HENRY MACY

Evening, Miss Amelia.

MACPHAIL

Miss Amelia.

RAINEY 1 & 2

Evening, Miss Amelia.

MISS AMELIA

(*Nods; grunts. Not unpleasantly, though; it is her
way*)

HENRY MACY

I come by. I thought . . . I come by.

RAINEY 1

. . . We said you been to the still.

MISS AMELIA (*Very deliberately*)

I been *thinking*.

RAINEY 2

(MISS AMELIA'S *remark is a known quantity*)

Oh-oh.

(RAINEY 1 *giggles*)

You been thinking on a new medicine? You making improvements on your Croup Cure?

MISS AMELIA (*Shakes her head*)

No.

RAINEY 1

You figuring on someone to sue, Miss Amelia? You found somebody you can bring suit against, Miss Amelia?

MISS AMELIA

No. (*Pause*) I been thinking on some way to get some silence out of you; I been figuring up a nice batch of poison to stop your foolish mouth.

(*The* RAINEY TWINS *giggle, laugh.* MACPHAIL *roars.* HENRY MACY *shakes his head, smiles*)

MISS AMELIA

(*Pushing* RAINEY 1 *roughly, but not angrily with her boot*)

That's what I been doing.

RAINEY 1

Oh, Miss Amelia, you wouldn't do that with me.

MACPHAIL

Best thing ever happen round here.

RAINEY 2

Poison me; you poison my brother, you poison me.

MISS AMELIA

Oblige you both.

MACPHAIL

Better idea yet.
(*A chuckle or two; a silence*)

MISS AMELIA
(*A silence.* To THEM *all*)
You come to buy liquor?

MACPHAIL

If you'd be so kind . . .

RAINEY 1

We all thirsty from the lack of rain.
(RAINEY 2 *giggles*)

MISS AMELIA (*After a long pause*)

I'll get some liquor.

HENRY MACY
(*Just as* MISS AMELIA *starts to turn, halting her*)
I see something coming.
(THEY *all look off, stage-left, where nothing is yet to be seen*)

RAINEY 1

It's a calf got loose.
(THEY *keep looking*)

MACPHAIL

No; no it ain't.
(THEY *keep looking*)

RAINEY 2

No; it's somebody's youngun.
(THEY *keep looking*)

HENRY MACY
(As a figure emerges from stage-left)

No . . . no.

MISS AMELIA *(Squinting)*

What is it then?

(COUSIN LYMON *moves into the lighted area near the porch; his clothes are dusty; he carries a tiny battered suitcase tied with a rope.* HE *is a dwarf; a hunchback.* HE *stops, suitcase still in hand;* HE *is out of breath)*

COUSIN LYMON

Evening. I am hunting for Miss Amelia Evans.

(The group neither replies nor nods; merely stares)

MISS AMELIA *(After a long pause)*

How come?

COUSIN LYMON

Because I am kin to her.

(The group looks at MISS AMELIA *to see her reaction)*

MISS AMELIA *(After a long pause)*

You lookin' for me. How do you mean "kin"?

COUSIN LYMON

Because . . . *(Uneasily, as if* HE *is about to cry, setting the suitcase down, but keeping hold of the handle)* Because my mother was Fanny Jesup and she came from Cheehaw. She left Cheehaw some thirty years ago when she married her first husband.

(RAINEY 1 giggles)

COUSIN LYMON

. . . and I am the son of Fanny's first husband. So that would make you and I . . . (*His voice trails off. With quick, bird-like gestures* HE *bends down, opens the suitcase*) I have a . . . (*Brings out a photograph*) . . . this is a picture of my mother and her half-sister.

> (HE *holds it out to* MISS AMELIA, *who does not take it.* MACPHAIL *does, examines it in the light*)

MACPHAIL
(After squinting at the photograph)

Why . . . what is this supposed to be! What are those . . . baby children? And so fuzzy you can't tell night from day. (HE *hands it towards* MISS AMELIA *who refuses it, keeping her gaze on* COUSIN LYMON. HE *hands the photograph back to the hunchback*) Where you come from?

COUSIN LYMON *(Uncertainly)*

I was . . . traveling.

> (RAINEY 2 *giggles contemptuously.* HENRY MACY *gets up, starts to leave*)

HENRY MACY
Night, Miss Amelia.

RAINEY 1
Where you going, Henry? Ain't you going to wait on your liquor?

RAINEY 2
Oh, no; Henry will sacrifice his thirst cause he is too squeamish; he don't want to be here when Miss Amelia boot this kind off her property. He don't want to be here for that.

HENRY MACY *(As* HE *exits)*
Night, Miss Amelia.

RAINEY 1

That right, Henry? You don't want to see Miss Amelia send this one flying?

> (HENRY MACY *exits, without commenting or turning.*
> COUSIN LYMON, *who has been waiting, apprehensively, finally sits down on the steps and suddenly begins to cry. No one moves;* THEY *watch him*)

RAINEY 2 *(Finally)*

Well, I'll be damned if he ain't a . . . look at him go! . . . I'll be damned if he ain't a regular crybaby.

RAINEY 1

He is a poor little thing.

MACPHAIL

Well, he is afflicted. There is some cause.

> (RAINEY 2 *loudly imitates* COUSIN LYMON's *crying.*
> MISS AMELIA *crosses the porch slowly but deliberately.* SHE *reaches* COUSIN LYMON *and stops, looking thoughtfully at him. Then, gingerly, with her right forefinger,* SHE *touches the hump on his back.* SHE *keeps her finger there until his crying lessens. Then,* SHE *removes her finger from his hump, takes a bottle from her hip pocket, wipes the top with the palm of her other hand, and offers it to him to drink*)

MISS AMELIA

Drink. *(Brief pause)* It will liven your gizzard.

RAINEY 1 *(To* COUSIN LYMON*)*

Hey there, you; better get your money up; Miss Amelia don't give liquor free. Unh-unh, you get your money up.

MISS AMELIA *(To* COUSIN LYMON*)*

Drink.

(COUSIN LYMON *stops crying and, rather like a snuf-
fling child, puts the bottle to his mouth and drinks.
When* HE *is done,* MISS AMELIA *takes the bottle,
washes her mouth with a small swallow, spits it out,
and then drinks. This done,* SHE *hands the bottle
back to* COUSIN LYMON. HE *takes it enthusiastically
To the others, as* SHE *moves to the store door)*

You want liquor? You get your money up.

(SHE *goes inside, takes three bottles from the counter.
The three men watch* COUSIN LYMON *as* HE *drinks.*
MISS AMELIA *returns with the liquor, gives a bottle to
each of the men, takes money. The men open the
bottles—which are corked—and take long, slow swal-
lows.* MISS AMELIA *near to* COUSIN LYMON)

MACPHAIL *(Music beginning)*

It is smooth liquor, Miss Amelia; I have never known you to
fail.

RAINEY 1

Yeah.

RAINEY 2

Yeah, sure is.

THE NARRATOR

*(Music under this speech. Maybe the lighting on
the scene alters slightly. The players drink, laugh,
ad lib, but softly under the following paragraph)*

The whiskey they drank that evening is important. Otherwise, it would be hard to account for what followed. Perhaps
without it there would never have been a cafe. For the liquor
of Miss Amelia has a special quality of its own. It is clean and
sharp on the tongue, but once down a man, it glows inside
him for a long time afterward. And that is not all. Things
that have gone unnoticed, thoughts that have been harbored

far back in the dark mind, are suddenly recognized and comprehended.

(*Laughter from the group here, more noticeable than usual*)

A man may suffer, or he may be spent with joy—but he has warmed his soul and seen the message hidden there.

(*Music ending; focus now back on porch scene*)

RAINEY 1

(*Leaning back; a quiet sound of deep satisfaction*)

Ohhhh—Whooooooo . . .

MACPHAIL (*After a pause*)

Yes; that *is* good.

MISS AMELIA

(*To* COUSIN LYMON, *after a pause*)

I don't know your name.

COUSIN LYMON

I'm Lymon Willis.

RAINEY 2 (*Softly, to no one*)

I am warm and dreamy.

MISS AMELIA

(*Rising, to* COUSIN LYMON)

Well, come on in. Some supper was left in the stove and you can eat.

(*The three* TOWNSMEN *look at* MISS AMELIA *and* COUSIN LYMON. RAINEY 1 *nudges* RAINEY 2. COUSIN LYMON *does not move*)

MISS AMELIA

I'll just warm up what's there.

(*As before, more or less*)

There is fried chicken; there are rootabeggars, collards and sweet potatoes.

COUSIN LYMON
(Stirring, shy and coy, almost like a young girl)
I am partial to collards—if they be cooked with sausage.

MISS AMELIA *(Pause)*
They be.
(RAINEY 2 *giggles softly)*

COUSIN LYMON
(Rising, facing MISS AMELIA*)*
I am partial to collards.

MISS AMELIA
(Moving toward the door)
Then bring your stuff.
(COUSIN LYMON *closes his suitcase, picks it up, stands on a step, looking at* MISS AMELIA, *still hesitant)*

COUSIN LYMON
(Softly, as if describing a glory)
. . . with sausages.

MISS AMELIA
There is a room for you upstairs . . . where you can sleep . . . when you are done eating.
(COUSIN LYMON *follows* MISS AMELIA *into the store, the interior of which fades, the front wall of the building takes its place.*
The three TOWNSMEN *sit for a moment. Music, softly)*

MACPHAIL *(Stirring)*
Well . . . *(Pause)* . . . home *(Rises)*

RAINEY 1
(To MACPHAIL *in some awe*)

I never seen nothing like that in my life. What she up to? Miss Amelia never invite people into her house . . . eat from her table. What she up to?

MACPHAIL (*Puzzled*)

Don't know.
(*Begins to cross, stage left. The* RAINEY TWINS *follow after*)

RAINEY 1

What is she up to, Stumpy? Hunh?

MACPHAIL (*Speeding up, exiting*)

Don't know.
(THE TWINS *stop, toward stage left, look back to the building*)

RAINEY 1

What is she up to? She never done a thing like that since . . .

RAINEY 2

Shhh! (*Giggles*) Can't talk about that.

RAINEY 1

Maybe . . . maybe she think there something in that suitcase of his. (*With some excitement*) Maybe she going to rob him! And then . . . and then kill him!

RAINEY 2 (*Giggles*)

Oh . . . hush. (*Giggles again*)

RAINEY 1
(As THEY *move off, stage left*)

I don't know . . . I don't know what she up to.

RAINEY 2 *(Expansively)*

I am warm and dreamy!

RAINEY 1 *(Shaking his head)*

I don't know.

> *(Lights slowly down to black, music under. Black for five seconds, chord held under, then lights up to bright day; brief, brisk morning music)*

HENRY MACY *enters, stage-left, stays there.* MISS AMELIA *comes out from the building, looks at the sky, goes to the pump in front of the building, washes her head, arms; does not dry—shakes off her arms; spies* HENRY MACY, *pauses; does not speak or nod.*

HENRY MACY

(A greeting that is a question)

Morning, Miss Amelia?

> *(*SHE *nods, waits.* HE *takes a step or two closer)*

You . . . you opening the store?

MISS AMELIA *(Squinting)*

You here to buy?

HENRY MACY

Why, no now; I just . . .

MISS AMELIA

Then I am closed.

HENRY MACY

Well . . . I just . . .

MISS AMELIA *(Fixing a sleeve)*

I am off to tend to some land I bought . . . up near Fork
Falls Road.

HENRY MACY *(Shyly)*

Land, Miss Amelia?

MISS AMELIA

Cotton. *(Pause)* You don't want nothing?
(Pause. HENRY MACY *shakes his head)*

MISS AMELIA

Then I am off.
*(*SHE *turns, moves stage-right. Two Townsladies,*
EMMA *and* MRS. PETERSON *enter from stage-right)*

EMMA *(In a portentous way)*

Morning, Miss Amelia.

MRS. PETERSON
(Timid; breathless)

Morning, Miss Amelia.
*(*THEY *stand;* MISS AMELIA *stands. The two* LADIES
cannot help but steal glances toward the building.
THEY *stand silently;* MISS AMELIA *scratches her leg)*

MISS AMELIA
(Not unfriendly, but not friendly)

You two want something?

MRS. PETERSON

Why . . . why whatever do you mean?

EMMA *(Significantly again)*

Just passing the time of day, Miss Amelia.

MISS AMELIA

You here to buy?

EMMA *(As before)*

Why, are you open today, Miss Amelia?

MISS AMELIA

Yes . . . or no?

MRS. PETERSON *(Flustered)*

Why . . . no; no.

MISS AMELIA

(Striding past them exiting)

I got business to tend to.

EMMA

(After her, but so SHE *cannot hear; really for* MRS.
PETERSON *and* HENRY MACY*)*

Oh! I'll bet you do. Have you foreclosed on someone, Miss
Amelia? You grabbed some more property on a debt? You
drove another poor, luckless soul out of his land?

        *(*MRS. PETERSON *tsks, rapidly, softly)*

Bet that's what she done.

HENRY MACY

Morning, ladies.

        (The THREE *meet toward center stage)*

EMMA

Henry Macy! Is it true? Is it true what I hear?

HENRY MACY *(Drawled)*

Why, I don't know, Emma. What is it you hear?

EMMA

Don't you sport with me! You know perfectly well what I hear . . . what the whole town hear.

HENRY MACY (*A small smile*)

Well, now, people hear a lot.

EMMA

Two nights ago? Here? You all sitting around, late, you men?

HENRY MACY

Well that is true; yes; we was sitting.

MRS. PETERSON (*Exasperated*)

Ohhhhhhhhhh.

EMMA

. . . and then up the road, out of the dark, come this broke-back, this runt? Some tiny thing claim to be kin to Miss Amelia?

HENRY MACY

Now is that what you hear?

EMMA

. . . and this twisted thing claim to be kin?

MRS. PETERSON
(*Almost whispered*)

. . . and he was took upstairs . . . and he ain't been seen since?

(HENRY MACY *shakes his head; laughs softly*)

EMMA (*Officiously*)

Well?

HENRY MACY (*Calmly; slowly*)

A brokeback come by . . . two nights ago . . . he claim to
be kin to Miss Amelia . . . Miss Amelia take him in . . .
feed him . . . offer him a bed.

(MRS. PETERSON *gasps with enthusiasm*)

EMMA (*To nail it down*)

And he ain't been seen since.

MRS. PETERSON

I knew it; I knew it.

HENRY MACY

You knew what?

MRS. PETERSON (*Helplessly*)

I . . . knew it.

(STUMPY MACPHAIL *enters, from stage-left, carrying a
lunch pail*)

EMMA (*To* MACPHAIL)

. . . And he ain't been seen since; morning.

MACPHAIL

Morning. Who ain't? Morning, Henry.

EMMA

Why, you know . . .

HENRY MACY

Morning, Stumpy.

MACPHAIL (*To* MRS. PETERSON)

Morning. (*To* EMMA) Who ain't?

EMMA *(Exasperated)*

Why, you know! That brokeback . . . that kind claim to be
kin to Miss Amelia.

MACPHAIL
(Scratching his head, looking toward building)

Oh . . . yeah, yeah.

MRS. PETERSON *(Proudly)*

And he ain't been seen since.

EMMA

Two days . . . no sign of . . . whatever it is.

HENRY MACY *(Weary)*

Oh, Emma . . .

MACPHAIL

Well, now; he may have took ill. He is afflicted.

EMMA *(Mysteriously)*

May. May not.

MRS. PETERSON

May not.

MACPHAIL

It ain't natural.

EMMA

It sure ain't.

HENRY MACY

He say he is kin.

EMMA

Miss Amelia got no kin!

MACPHAIL

Who can have kin like what come 't'other night? That be kin to no one.

EMMA

Whatever he be, Miss Amelia been took in.

HENRY MACY

Miss Amelia ain't known to be soft-hearted.

EMMA *(Triumphantly)*

In the head, then!

MACPHAIL

I say she fed him, sent him on.

HENRY MACY

You told me she give him a bed.

MACPHAIL

She *say*. That don't mean nothing.
    (Enter RAINEY 1, *he, too, with a lunch pail. Trailing behind him,* MERLIE RYAN.
    To RAINEY 1)
That don't mean nothing; do it?

RAINEY 1

What don't mean nothing?

MACPHAIL

Miss Amelia *say* she give the brokeback a bed don't mean he stay.

RAINEY 1 *(With great relish)*
Ain't nobody seen him, hunh? Well now, where could he be?

EMMA
(To MRS. PETERSON, *who breathes agreement)*
Just what I *say.*

MERLIE RYAN
I know what Miss Amelia done.

EMMA *(Dismissing him)*
Hunh, you—you queer-headed old thing.

MACPHAIL
(With a gesture to quiet EMMA: *very interested)*
What; what she done?
*(*RAINEY 1 *giggles)*

MERLIE RYAN
I know what Miss Amelia done.
*(*RAINEY 1 *giggles again)*

EMMA
Well, what?

MRS. PETERSON
What?

MERLIE RYAN
(As if remembering a message to be given)
I know what Miss Amelia done: She murdered that man for
something in that suitcase.
   *(*HENRY MACY *snorts dismissal;* RAINEY 1 *giggles;*
   MACPHAIL *whistles; the* LADIES *gasp)*
She murdered that man for something in that suitcase. She

cut his body up, and she bury him in the swamp. (*As before from the* OTHERS) I know what Miss Amelia done?
  (*Maybe the* LADIES *stare at the building, move back from it*)

HENRY MACY
(*Ridiculing the idea*)

Oh, now . . .

MRS. PETERSON

I knew it; I knew it . . .

EMMA
(*With great, slow nods of her head*)

So that what she done.

MERLIE RYAN (*Sing-song*)

That what she done; that what she done.
  (RAINEY 1 *giggles*)

HENRY MACY (*To* RAINEY 1)

You tell him this? You put these things in his head?

RAINEY 1
(*So we do not know if* HE *is serious or not*)

Me? Tell a thing like that to Crazy Merlie here? Why, Henry; you know me better'n that.

EMMA

Buried him in the swamp.

MACPHAIL

It ain't beyond reason.

HENRY MACY (*Angry*)

It ain't likely!

MERLIE RYAN

I know what Miss Amelia done.

(RAINEY 1 *giggles*)
(Barely audible chatter from those on stage during the following)

THE NARRATOR *(Music under it)*

And so it went that whole day. A midnight burial in the swamp, the dragging of Miss Amelia through the streets of the town on the way to prison . . .

(THREE OTHER TOWNSMEN *enter, join in*)

. . . the squabbles over what would happen to her property —all told in hushed voices and repeated with some fresh and weird detail.

(Lighting moves toward evening: MISS AMELIA *enters, stage-right, takes brief note of the townspeople, moves into the building)*

And when it came toward evening, and Miss Amelia returned from her business, and they saw that there were no bloodstains on her anywhere, the consternation grew.

MISS AMELIA

Well, quite a gathering.

*(It becomes dark, now. The townsmen—*HENRY MACY, MACPHAIL, THE RAINEY TWINS, MERLIE RYAN *and the* THREE TOWNSMEN, RAINEY 2 *having entered from stage-left at the beginning of this lighting change—have moved to the porch of the building, are sitting or standing with* HENRY MACY *off to one side of the group . . . stage-right.* EMMA *and* MRS. PETERSON *have been joined by two other women, and are in a group, stage-left, watching the porch, watching the men)*

THE NARRATOR

And dark came on. It was just past eight o'clock, and still

nothing had happened. But there was silent agreement among the men that this night would not pass with the mystery still unsolved. There is a time beyond which questions may not stay unanswered. So, the men had gathered on Miss Amelia's porch, and Miss Amelia had gone into the room she kept as an office.

(*Lights on* MISS AMELIA *in the office*)

FIRST TOWNSMAN (*To* SECOND)

What she doin'?

SECOND TOWNSMAN

Don't know. I don't know.

MERLIE RYAN

I know what she done. She murdered that man for somethin' . . .

MACPHAIL

Shhh.

HENRY MACY

Hush, Merlie!

(BOTH RAINEYS *giggle*)

FIRST TOWNSMAN

What we gonna do?

RAINEY 1

We goin' in?

MACPHAIL (*Rising portentously*)

Yup; we goin' in. Henry?

HENRY MACY (*After a pause*)

All right.

(*The* MEN *rise, file slowly into the store; the* WOMEN, *taking this as a sign, move, with sotto voce comments, toward the porch. The* MEN *move silently, keeping fairly close to the walls, keeping a distance from both* MISS AMELIA's *office and from the stairs, stage-center-rear.*

Maybe there is a high, soft sustained chord of music here, ending abruptly with a sound from the top of the stairs. The MEN *turn toward the sound.*

COUSIN LYMON *descends the stairs, slowly, one at a time—imperiously, like a great hostess.* HE *is no longer ragged;* HE *is clean;* HE *wears his little coat, but neat and mended, a red and black checkered shirt, knee breeches, black stockings, shoes laced up over the ankles, and a great lime green shawl, with fringe, which almost touches the ground. The effect is somehow regal . . . or papal. The room is as still as death.* COUSIN LYMON *walks to the center of the room; the* MEN *move back a little.* HE *stares at them, one after the other, down to up, slowly, craning his neck to see their faces.* RAINEY 2 *giggles, but there is some terror in it*)

COUSIN LYMON

(*After* HE *has examined the* MEN; *as if* HE *had heard some piece of unimportant news, which* HE *dismisses*)

Evenin'.

(HE *seats himself on a barrel, quite center, and takes from a pocket a snuff-box. There is an intake of breath from* SOME *of the* MEN)

MACPHAIL

(*Daring to move a step closer*)

What is it you have there?

FIRST TOWNSMAN

Yeah; what is that, Peanut?

SECOND TOWNSMAN

Why, that is Miss Amelia's snuffbox . . . belonged to her father.

MACPHAIL

What is it you have there?

COUSIN LYMON
(Sharply; mischievously)

What is this? Why, this is a lay-low . . . to catch meddlers.

SECOND TOWNSMAN

It *is* her snuffbox. Belonged to her father.

COUSIN LYMON *(After taking snuff)*

This is not proper snuff; this is sugar and cocoa.
(Silence from the MEN; MISS AMELIA *can be heard whistling softly to herself)*
The very teeth in my head have always tasted sour to me; that is the reason why I take this kind of sweet snuff.

MACPHAIL *(To get it straight)*

It *is* Miss Amelia's snuffbox.

COUSIN LYMON *(Almost arrogantly)*

Yes?

HENRY MACY

It is natural enough.

COUSIN LYMON
(Swinging on him; not unfriendly—objective)

Who are you?

HENRY MACY (*Kindly*)

I am Henry Macy.

COUSIN LYMON

I remember; when I come. How old are you?
   (*An exchange of glances among the* OTHER MEN; *one
   or two words*)

HENRY MACY

I am forty-seven.

COUSIN LYMON (*Swinging his legs*)

Where you work?

HENRY MACY

The mill.

COUSIN LYMON (*To* MACPHAIL)

And you!

MACPHAIL

I . . .

COUSIN LYMON

Who are *you*?

RAINEY 2

That Stumpy MacPhail.
         (*Giggles*)

COUSIN LYMON

How old are you?

MACPHAIL

I am . . . thirty-eight.

RAINEY 1

He work in the mill, too.

COUSIN LYMON
(*Igoring* RAINEY 1; *to* MACPHAIL)

You married, Stumpy MacPhail?

RAINEY 2

Oh, is he!
(*A* COUPLE *of the* MEN *laugh gently*)

MACPHAIL (*Retaining his dignity*)

I am married. Yes.

COUSIN LYMON
(*A small, pleased child*)

Is your wife fat?
(*Whoops of laughter from the* MEN, *which bring
the* WOMEN *hovering to the door*)

MACPHAIL
(*Embarrassed, but by the attention, not the fact*)

She is . . . ample.
(*More laughter*)

COUSIN LYMON (*To* RAINEY TWINS)

And you two giggling things . . . who are *you*?

FIRST TOWNSMAN

Them is the Rainey twins . . .

SECOND TOWNSMAN
(*Indicating* MERLIE RYAN)

And this here is Merlie Ryan . . .

COUSIN LYMON
(With a sweep of his hand)

Come in, ladies!

(The TOWNSWOMEN *enter, the introductions become
general, simultaneous. The* THREE TOWNSMEN *use
names such as* HASTY MALONE, ROSSER CLINE, *and*
HENRY FORD CRIMP. EMMA *is* EMMA HALE. *The chatter is general; and while there is a lot of talk and
some laughter, there is still tension, and people tend
to look at* COUSIN LYMON *out of the corners of their
eyes and keep a formal distance—as if* HE *were a
Martian, a friendly Martian, but still a Martian.
There are now* TWELVE TOWNSPEOPLE *in the store.
Through the general chatter we hear, specifically,
things like the following)*

RAINEY 1

When you come up the road t'other night . . . I swore it
were a calf got loose.

RAINEY 2 *(Qualifying)*

It were so dark.

HENRY MACY

It is a pleasure to have you visiting.

EMMA

This lime green scarf is pretty.

MRS. PETERSON

Oh, yes; yes, it look well on you.

COUSIN LYMON
(To MRS. PETERSON*)*

I will not bite you. *(Snaps his teeth at her)* Grrr!

MRS. PETERSON (*Almost fainting*)
Oh! Oh!

MERLIE RYAN
Know what I thought she done? . . . Know what I thought
happened to the brokeback? . . .

HENRY MACY & MACPHAIL
Hush. You be still.

RAINEY 2
. . . and I thought it were someone's youngun . . .

RAINEY 1
It were so dark.

COUSIN LYMON
Well, it were not.

RAINEY 2
No; it were not.

(*Giggles*)

RAINEY 1
It were dark.
> (*Groups have formed, and the conversation does not
> hinge solely on* COUSIN LYMON. *Perhaps music has
> been used judiciously throughout this ad lib scene.
> The door to the office swings open, and* MISS AMELIA
> *enters the store. As the* TOWNSPEOPLE *see her, their
> conversation trails off, until there is silence.* MISS
> AMELIA *stands for a moment, taking everything in,
> glances at* COUSIN LYMON *and smiles, briefly, shyly,
> then leans her elbows back on the counter*)

MISS AMELIA (*Quietly*)

Does anyone want waiting on?

>   (*A brief pause, which* HENRY MACY *breaks*)

HENRY MACY

Why, yes, Miss Amelia . . . if you have some liquor . . .

>   (*This serves as a dam-break, and* SEVERAL *of the* MEN
>   *ad lib agreement, and the general chatter starts
>   again.*
>   *Music from now until the end of the scene.*
>   MISS AMELIA *turns, goes behind the counter, gets
>   bottles, serves the* MEN, *takes money*)

THE NARRATOR (*Over the talk*)

What happened at this moment was not ordinary. While the men of the town could count on Miss Amelia for their liquor, it was a rule she had that they must drink it outside her premises—and there was no feeling of joy in the transaction: after getting his liquor, a man would have to drink it on the porch, or guzzle it on the street, or walk off into the night. But at this moment, Miss Amelia broke her rule, and the men could drink in her store. More than that, she furnished glasses and opened two boxes of crackers so that they were there hospitably in a platter on the counter and anyone who wished could take one free.

>   (*Suitable action under the above, general chatter
>   continuing*)

Now, this was the beginning of the cafe. It was as simple as that. There was a certain timidness, for people in this town were unused to gathering together in any number for the sake of pleasure. But, it was the beginning.

>   (*The sounds continue.* MISS AMELIA *moves to where*
>   COUSIN LYMON *is sitting*)

MISS AMELIA

Cousin Lymon, will you have your liquor straight, or warmed
in a pan with water on the stove?
(*A slight lessening in the general conversation in attention to this*)

COUSIN LYMON

If you please, Amelia . . . if you please, I'll have it warmed.
(*Some general consternation*)

EMMA

(*A half-whisper, to anyone, as* MISS AMELIA, *smiling
secretly, moves off to do* COUSIN LYMON's *bidding*)
Did you hear that? He called her *Amelia!* He said *Amelia!*

MRS. PETERSON
(*Breathless, as usual*)
Why, it is *Miss* Amelia to . . . to everyone.

EMMA

And *he* called her *Amelia.*

THIRD TOWNSMAN

Her Daddy called her . . . Little. He called her Little.
(RAINEY 2 *giggles*)

RAINEY 1

Some Little!

EMMA (*Unable to get over it*)
Did you hear it? He called her Amelia.
(*In another area,* HENRY MACY, MACPHAIL *and* MERLIE
RYAN *are gathered*)

MACPHAIL

I ain't see Miss Amelia like this. There is something puzzling to her face.

HENRY MACY
(*Looking at her;* SHE *is oblivious to all but* COUSIN LYMON)

Well . . . it may be she is happy.

MACPHAIL (*Uncertain*)

It may be.

MERLIE RYAN

I know; I know what it is.

HENRY MACY

Oh, now, Merlie . . .

MERLIE RYAN

I know what it is . . . Miss Amelia in love. That what it is.
(*Only* HENRY MACY *and* MACPHAIL *have heard this*)

MACPHAIL
(*As if* HE *is being joshed*)

Ohhhhhhhh . . .

HENRY MACY

Hush, now, Merlie . . .

MERLIE RYAN

Miss Amelia in love. Miss Amelia in love.
(*Music and* CROWD *louder, general party. Interior of the store dims, becomes invisible during the next speech, the exterior becoming visible, in the darkness and moonlight*)

THE NARRATOR

And so it went. This opening of the cafe came to an end at
midnight. Everyone said goodbye to everyone else in a friendly
fashion . . . and soon, everything—all the town, in fact—
was dark and silent. And so ended three days and nights in
which had come the arrival of a stranger, an unholy holiday,
and the start of the cafe.

(Dim to blackness. MUSIC *holds)*

*Daylight—toward evening—comes up; only the ex-
terior of the cafe is visible save directly below, as
indicated. No one, narrator excepted, is on stage.
Music up and under.*

THE NARRATOR

Now time must pass. Four years . . . Time passes quickly in
this section of the country; you breathe in and it is summer;
out, and it is autumn; in again, out, and a year has gone by.
Only the seasons change, but they are so regular in their turning that four years can pass . . . *(Pause)* . . . like that. The
hunchback continued to live with Miss Amelia. The cafe ex-
panded in a gradual way, and Miss Amelia began to sell her
liquor by the drink, and some tables were brought into the
store, and there were customers every evening, and on Saturday nights a great crowd. The place was a store no longer but
had become a proper cafe, and was open every evening from
six until twelve o'clock. Things once done were accepted.

*(*MISS AMELIA *and* COUSIN LYMON *emerge, sit on the
steps)*

And Cousin Lymon's presence in Miss Amelia's house, his
sleeping in her dead father's room, was passed by, save by a
few, women mostly, whose minds had darker corners than
they dared dream of. And the cafe was welcomed by every-

one but the minister's wife, who was a secret drinker and felt
more alone than ever. Four years have passed . . .

COUSIN LYMON
(As MISS AMELIA *massages his shoulders)*
Slowly, Amelia, slowly.

MISS AMELIA *(Amused tolerance)*
Yes, Cousin Lymon.

COUSIN LYMON
That do feel good, Amelia.

MISS AMELIA
You have not grown stronger; you are still so pitiful.

COUSIN LYMON
I am not a big person, Amelia.

MISS AMELIA
Now, I think your head *has* got bigger . . . and your hunch,
too . . .

COUSIN LYMON *(Pulls away; surly)*
Leave me be.

MISS AMELIA
But your legs, as thin as ever . . . grasshopper . . .

COUSIN LYMON
(A tone of command)
Amelia! *(A sudden giggle)* Course, you could always figger up
a new medicine for me . . . one turn me into a giant; you
could do that.

MISS AMELIA (*Affectionately*)

You enough trouble big as you are. Don't know what I'd do with you normal size.

COUSIN LYMON (*Greatly amused*)

Though there be a danger you make me a growin' medicine, since you so particular with your remedies you try 'em out on yourself first . . .

MISS AMELIA (*Laughs*)

Hush, you.

COUSIN LYMON

. . . you make me a growin' medicine, an' it work we gonna have you in the treetops, birds nestin' in you, an' . . .

MISS AMELIA (*Gently*)

Ain't no medicine gonna make you grow, Cousin Lymon.

COUSIN LYMON (*Briefly serious*)

I know that, Amelia. (*Giggling again*) Only thing happen, you make up a new remedy be you try it out on yourself an' you spend the next two days hustlin' to the privy . . .

MISS AMELIA (*To stop him*)

Well, you gotta try your medicine on yourself first, you be any good at doctorin'.

COUSIN LYMON (*Giggles*)

I know . . . but it's funny.

MISS AMELIA

An' all ailments is centered in the bowel.

COUSIN LYMON

Oh?

MISS AMELIA
Yes.

COUSIN LYMON
(Mischievous scoffing)
Do that be so, Amelia?

MISS AMELIA
Yes.

COUSIN LYMON
Well, your remedies *do* affect the bowel, no doubt there. Surprisin' anyone die in these parts.

MISS AMELIA
People die here same as anywhere.

COUSIN LYMON *(Still mischievous)*
What do they die of, Amelia? Ain't your medicine, now . . .

MISS AMELIA
People die of natural causes. Like anywhere.

COUSIN LYMON
What is the natural cause, Amelia?

MISS AMELIA
(At a loss first; then . . .)
. . . dyin'.

COUSIN LYMON
(As if a great truth has been revealed)
Oh.

COUSIN LYMON
(*A tone of command*)

Amelia! (*A small silence, then* HE *continues in a cajoling tone*) As tomorrow is Sunday, Amelia, you gonna drive us into Cheehaw to the movie show? Or, maybe we can go to the fair. There is a fair which is out beyond . . .

MISS AMELIA

We will go . . . we will go . . . somewhere.

COUSIN LYMON

To the fair, Amelia.

MISS AMELIA

We will go . . . somewhere.
(COUSIN LYMON *pulls away again, dead-spoiled, pouting, moves a few feet away*)
Cousin Lymon?

COUSIN LYMON (*Imperiously*)

Your father's bed is too big for my size, Amelia; I am not comfortable in a bed that size.

MISS AMELIA (*Laughing*)

Oh, now . . .

COUSIN LYMON (*Greatly petulant*)

I said I am not at ease in a ten acre bed. Have one made for me; have a bed made for me that I can sleep comfortable in.

MISS AMELIA
(*Attempting a light tone*)

I will have a bed made for you, Cousin Lymon, just to your size, and it can be used for you as a coffin some day.

COUSIN LYMON
(Rising; furious; screaming)

I AM SLEEPING IN A COFFIN NOW! I AM SLEEPING IN YOUR FA-
THER'S COFFIN. *(Softer, whining again)* I want a small bed,
Amelia. I want a bed my size.

MISS AMELIA *(Placating)*

Yes; yes.

COUSIN LYMON

And . . . and I want to go in the Ford tomorrow . . . to
Cheehaw . . . to the movie show, and . . .

MISS AMELIA
(Quietly correcting him)

You want to go to the *fair*.

COUSIN LYMON *(Imperious again)*

Either way; don't matter.

MISS AMELIA *(A slightly sad smile)*

No; don't matter.

COUSIN LYMON
(Mysterious and intensely curious)

Amelia . . . in the parlor upstairs there is that curio cabinet
that had that snuff-box you gave me I admired so when I first
came.

MISS AMELIA *(Affirming this)*

Yes, Cousin Lymon, there be.

COUSIN LYMON

Well, that cabinet has in it some *other* things that I have
become curious about, and I would like to ask you about
them.

MISS AMELIA
(Suddenly defensive, her eyes narrowing)
You go in there? You rummage about in that curio cabinet?

COUSIN LYMON
(His eyes narrowing, too)
Why, Amelia, it is a curio cabinet, and I am a curious little person; besides, Amelia, you got no secrets from me.
(HE goes into a pocket, takes out a small velvet box, at the sight of which MISS AMELIA makes a half grab, but COUSIN LYMON moves away)
And now, I have found this tiny velvet box, and if I open it up . . . *(Does so)* . . . what do I see?

MISS AMELIA *(Blushing)*
You give that here.

COUSIN LYMON
What do I see? *(Pause)* Hmm? What do I see?
(Looks to MISS AMELIA, who still blushes and will not look at either him or the box)
I see two small little grey stones, and I wonder to myself "What do they be? Why has Amelia kept these stones?" What do they be, Amelia?
(MISS AMELIA mumbles something at last, which we cannot hear)
Hmm? I did not hear you, Amelia.

MISS AMELIA *(Shyer than ever)*
They be . . .

COUSIN LYMON *(Enjoying it greatly)*
Yes? Yes?

MISS AMELIA *(Finally)*
They be . . . I were in great pain, years back, and I went

COUSIN LYMON
(After a brief, almost unkind hesitation; gifting her)
Why no, Amelia, you may have it. It were your father's and he were dear to you.

MISS AMELIA
(With a remembering smile)
He were. Law, I remember when I were little, I slept and slept. I'd go to bed just as the lamp was turned on and sleep —why, I'd sleep like I was drowned in warm axle grease. Then come daybreak Papa would walk in and put his hand down on my shoulder. "Get stirring, Little," he would say. Then later he would holler up the stairs from the kitchen when the stove was hot. "Fried grits," he would holler. "White meat and gravy. Ham and eggs." And I'd run down the stairs and dress by the hot stove while he was washing up out at the pump. Then off we'd go to the still, or maybe . . .

COUSIN LYMON
The grits we had this morning was poor; fried too quick so that the inside never heated.

MISS AMELIA
And when Papa would run off the liquor in those days . . .

COUSIN LYMON
You know I don't like grits lest they be done exactly right. You know I have told you many times, Amelia . . .

MISS AMELIA
. . . or when he would take me with him when he buried the barrels . . .

COUSIN LYMON
I say: the grits we had this morning was poor.

MISS AMELIA

. . . an' we would go, an' . . . all right, Cousin Lymon; I will take more care with them.

COUSIN LYMON

You loved your poppa, didn't you, Amelia?

MISS AMELIA

I . . .

COUSIN LYMON

You can say it.

MISS AMELIA *(Finally)*

Course I loved my poppa. Momma dyin' as she did, birthin' me . . .

COUSIN LYMON

You were normal size, Amelia? You a regular baby size when you born?

MISS AMELIA
(Laughing amazement)

Course I was, Cousin Lymon.

COUSIN LYMON

Course you were.

MISS AMELIA

. . . an' . . . an' poppa an' me, we'd take long trips together . . .

COUSIN LYMON

Into Cheehaw? Or to the fair sometimes?

MISS AMELIA

Yes . . . an' sometimes beyond. Way beyond. We'd take long trips.

COUSIN LYMON

And I found this Amelia—
> (HE *goes into a pocket, takes out a small velvet box,*
> *at the sight of which* MISS AMELIA *makes a half grab,*
> *but* COUSIN LYMON *moves away*)

I have found this tiny velvet box, and if I open it up . . .
(Does so) . . . what do I see?

MISS AMELIA *(Blushing)*

You give that here.

COUSIN LYMON

What do I see? *(Pause)* Hmm? What do I see?
> (*Looks to* MISS AMELIA, *who still blushes and will*
> *not look at either him or the box*)

I see two small little grey stones, and I wonder to myself
"What do they be? Why has Amelia kept these stones?"
What do they be, Amelia?
> (MISS AMELIA *mumbles something at last, which we*
> *cannot hear*)

Hmm? I did not hear you, Amelia.

MISS AMELIA *(Shyer than ever)*

They be . . .

COUSIN LYMON *(Enjoying it greatly)*

Yes? Yes?

MISS AMELIA *(Finally)*

They be . . . I were in great pain, years back, and I went
into Cheehaw, to the doctor there—I couldn't figure the pain,
and none of my remedies worked for it—and I went to the

doctor there and . . . (*In great embarrassment*) . . . those be my kidney stones. (*A fair silence*) Now, give 'em here.

COUSIN LYMON
(*Examining the stones*)
So that is what they be.

MISS AMELIA
Give them here, now.

COUSIN LYMON
I admire these, Amelia. You ain't given me a present in the longest time now. You give me these as a present. Yes?

MISS AMELIA
(*Can't help but laugh*)
But what would you do with them Cousin Lymon?

COUSIN LYMON
I have always admired . . . I have always wanted a great gold chain across my vest, and you could get me a great gold chain for across my vest, and you could have these hung from it. Oh, Amelia, I would love that so. I would so love that.
(MISS AMELIA *laughs blushingly*)
Oh, I would.

MISS AMELIA
Unh-hunh; yes, if you want it, Cousin Lymon.

COUSIN LYMON
(*Quite coldly*)
Oh, Amelia, I do love you so.

MISS AMELIA
(*With some awkward gesture: kicking the dirt off a boot, maybe*)

Humf! Those are words I don't wanna hear. (*Pause*) Understand?

COUSIN LYMON
(*A too-eager schoolboy*)

Yes, Amelia!

MISS AMELIA (*After a silence*)

I am fond of you, Cousin Lymon.
(*Music begins here, softly*)

THE NARRATOR

Ah, Amelia, I do love you so. Now, was that true? Well, we will find out. But it is true that Miss Amelia loved Cousin Lymon, for he was kin to her, and Miss Amelia had, for many years, before the arrival of Cousin Lymon, lived a solitary life. And, too, there are many kinds of love . . . as we shall find out. But this is how they talked, and was one of the ways in which Miss Amelia showed her love for Cousin Lymon . . . her fondness. In fact, there was only one part of her life that she did not want Cousin Lymon to share with her . . . to know about; and it concerned a man named Marvin Macy. It was a name that never crossed her lips . . . a name that no one in the town dared mention in her presence . . . the name Marvin Macy.

The scene changes slowly to dark. MISS AMELIA *and* COUSIN LYMON *rise, go indoors. Under* THE NARRATOR's *next speech the lights rise on the interior of the cafe, revealing it full of* TOWNSPEOPLE, *sitting around tables, drinking, or standing, buying, etc. Saturday night is in full swing. Everyone is there.* STUMPY MACPHAIL *and one of the* TOWNSMEN *are playing checkers; the* RAINEY TWINS *are at separate places, and* THEY *glower at each other occasionally.* HENRY MACY *is at a table by himself, downstage;* HE *is drinking and* HE *does not look happy. Music continues.*

THE NARRATOR

We come now to a night of terrible importance, the beginning of a series of events which will result in calamity and great sadness. It looks to be a Saturday night like any other since the cafe has opened, but the great and terrible events of a person's life occur most often in the most commonplace of circumstances.

(Music out.

Cafe scene up full, general chatter. COUSIN LYMON *mills around the* GUESTS. MISS AMELIA *enters, from the kitchen, bearing a handwritten sign with the legend, "Chicken dinner tonite—twenty cents")*

MISS AMELIA
(Tacking the sign up)
For them of you as can't read . . . Chicken dinner tonight . . . twenty cents.
(General approval; SOME PEOPLE *move to the kitchen to be served. It must be understood that there is ad lib conversation all throughout this scene)*
It's in the kitchen. Pay on the bar and get it yourselves.
*(*SHE *moves to where* HENRY MACY *sits)*
What ails you?

HENRY MACY *(Half rising)*
Miss Amelia?

MISS AMELIA
What ails you tonight, Henry?

HENRY MACY *(Obviously lying)*

Why . . . why, nothing, Miss Amelia. Nothing.

MISS AMELIA

Then you better eat.

HENRY MACY

No, no; I got a drink here, Miss Amelia; I will sit with it.

MISS AMELIA
(Still sits, regarding him)

Suit yourself.

COUSIN LYMON
(To STUMPY MACPHAIL*)*

And I walked to Rotten Lake today to fish, and on the way I stepped over what appeared at first to be a big fallen tree. But then as I stepped over I felt something stir and I taken this second look and there I was straddling this here alligator long as from the front door to the kitchen and thicker than a hog.

(STUMPY MACPHAIL *and* SEVERAL *of the* OTHERS *laugh goodnaturedly*)

STUMPY MACPHAIL

Sure you did, peanut. Sure.

COUSIN LYMON

I did. I did. And . . . and I looked down at him, and I . . .

MACPHAIL

. . . and you picked him up by his big ugly tail, and you swung him around your shoulder, and you flung him over the . . .

COUSIN LYMON *(Superior)*

All right, you just go look over at Rotten Lake sometime, smarty!

MISS AMELIA
(Smiling over to COUSIN LYMON*)*

You tell 'em.
(Now back to HENRY MACY*)*
Still not talkin'? Not eating? An' nothin' ails you, and you're just gonna sit there drinkin'. Right?

HENRY MACY

That's right, Miss Amelia.

MISS AMELIA
(Nods knowingly again)

All right.

COUSIN LYMON
(Having moved to where RAINEY 1 *is sitting)*

And how are you tonight?

RAINEY 1
(Glowering at RAINEY 2, *who returns his glower)*

Just dandy.

COUSIN LYMON
(Determined to make mischief)

Ohhhhh, and I see your brother is just dandy, too.

RAINEY 1

I don't know who you mean.

COUSIN LYMON

Why, I mean your lookalike.

RAINEY 1 *(Greatly indignant)*

Humf! That one!

RAINEY 2
(To COUSIN LYMON; HE *too indignant)*
Don't you go talkin' to that noaccount. He rob the hump off
your back quick as look at you.

COUSIN LYMON
(Marches over to RAINEY 2; *swipes at him, snarls, almost)*
You mean to say your brother is some kind of wizard? That
what you mean to say?

MISS AMELIA
(Still sitting, but concerned)
Cousin Lymon . . . ?

COUSIN LYMON
(Stamping back to RAINEY 1)
That what he mean to say? That what your noaccount
brother saying? He some kind of wizard?

RAINEY 2 *(So* ALL *will hear)*
I don't mean that. I mean that thievin' nogood over there'll
steal you blind before you know it.

RAINEY 1 *(Rising)*
I ain't no thief!

COUSIN LYMON
(Mischief again, coming between the BROTHERS)
Oh, now now now. You talked to him; I caught you: you
talked to your own brother.

RAINEY 1 *(Angry)*

I talked *on* him; I said I ain't no thief. I didn't talk *to* him.

COUSIN LYMON

My, my; two years now you two ain't spoke a word to each other; not a word in two whole years.

RAINEY 2

HE STOLE MY KNIFE!

RAINEY 1

I NEVER STOLE NOBODY'S KNIFE!
    (THEY *glare, subside.* COUSIN LYMON *moves to* MISS AMELIA)

COUSIN LYMON

Now, ain't that something, Amelia: These two not speaking to one another for more'n two years now over six inches of sharp steel? Ain't that something?

MISS AMELIA

Some people been killed for less.
    (COUSIN LYMON *chases* HENRIETTA FORD CRIMP JR. *around a table*)

MISS AMELIA

Leave that kid be. She been sick. *(Rises)* I'm eatin'. Cousin Lymon, can I bring you your dinner?

COUSIN LYMON

My appetite is poor tonight; there is a sourness in my mouth.

MISS AMELIA

Just a pick: the breast, the liver and the heart.

COUSIN LYMON
(Sweet-spoiled; sitting at the table with HENRY
MACY)
All right, Amelia, if you will do that for me.

MISS AMELIA
Henry?

HENRY MACY
No, Miss Amelia . . . thank you. I will stay with your good
liquor.

MISS AMELIA
(Walking to the kitchen)
Ain't like you, Henry.

COUSIN LYMON
(Imitating MISS AMELIA)
Ain't like you, Henry. What ails you, Henry Macy?

HENRY MACY
Nothin'! Now don't you start in, too!

COUSIN LYMON
Oooohhhh . . . Lawl

HENRY MACY
Just . . . leave it be.

COUSIN LYMON
Now, that ain't polite, Henry . . .

HENRY MACY
(A quiet warning; a little drunk)
Look, runt; go pick on someone your own size, hear?

MACPHAIL

Yeah, go back fight another flock o' alligators or whatever they was.

COUSIN LYMON
(TO STUMPY MACPHAIL)

You go on out to Rotten Lake now, and you see!
(EMMA *and* MRS. PETERSON *emerge from the kitchen, carrying plates; call back to* MISS AMELIA *in the kitchen)*

EMMA *(Her mouth full)*

Real fine chicken, Miss Amelia!

MRS. PETERSON

Oh, yes, a good bird . . . it is, Miss Amelia.

EMMA *(Still shouting)*

Real fine. *(Then sotto voce, to* MRS. PETERSON) Probably stole them chickens off some poor tenant farmer out near . . .

MRS. PETERSON

Ooooooohhhh, *Emma* . . .

EMMA

. . . or maybe somebody behind on a loan to her, she walk in an' say, "I'll take all your birds." That's what. Somethin' like that.

MRS. PETERSON *(Whispering)*
Emma.

EMMA *(Loud)*

Wouldn't put it past her.

COUSIN LYMON
(As THEY *pass him, barks at* EMMA*)*
WARF! WARF!

*(*SEVERAL PEOPLE *laugh)*

EMMA
(As MRS. PETERSON *squeals, jumps)*
You stop that, runt. I'll knock you clear into next week!

COUSIN LYMON
*(Raises his hands like a puppy's paws, whimpers a
moment; then)*
FATTY! You fat thing!

EMMA
(Looming above COUSIN LYMON, *as* MISS AMELIA
emerges from the kitchen with two plates)
FAT: Well, fat is better'n twisted you miserable little
runt . . . !

MISS AMELIA *(A command)*
EMMA HALE!

*(*EMMA *subsides, moves to a table)*

EMMA
(Not to MISS AMELIA, *but for her ears)*
They is some good cafes in these parts, I hear, where they
is not monkeys crawling around the floor; where the owners'
pets is not . . .

MISS AMELIA
(Setting a plate down before COUSIN LYMON *and
one at her own place)*
That'll do now.

MRS. PETERSON
(Whispered, breathless)
Emma, you *know* you mustn't . . .

MISS AMELIA
Them people oughta go to them cafes; if they ain't careful
they won't be welcome no more in *this* cafe.
(To COUSIN LYMON*)*
Eat.

COUSIN LYMON
(Sweet in victory and vindication, looking toward
EMMA*)*
Thank you, Amelia. And they is *some* cafes, I hear, where
they do not allow just *any*body to come in an' . . .

MISS AMELIA
(Silencing him, too, but kindly)
All right now. Eat.
*(*THEY *fall to; the general cafe conversation continues, lessens a bit, perhaps, for our attention should
move outside, stage-left, where the figure of a man
appears. It is* MARVIN MACY. HE *stands, gazing at the
cafe, begins whittling, all the while staring at the
cafe, and whistling softly.*
(To COUSIN LYMON*)*
You was hungry after all.

COUSIN LYMON
(Shovelling food into his mouth)
It would seem. But only for the delicacies. Like you choose
'em.

*(*HENRY MACY *clears his throat, makes as if to speak
of something difficult, but stops)*

MISS AMELIA

Henry Macy, if you gonna sit here all night, and drink liquor, and . . .

COUSIN LYMON (*Gleefully*)

Bet he got a secret.
(*Throughout the following, the cafe conversations grow quiet; eventually, when indicated, cease entirely*)

MISS AMELIA

You got a secret, Henry?

COUSIN LYMON

Bet he do.

HENRY MACY (*Finally*)

I . . . I got a letter last week, Miss Amelia.

MISS AMELIA
(*After a brief pause; unsurprised at the news*)

Yeah?

HENRY MACY

It were . . . it were a letter from my brother.
(*Noticeable lessening in the cafe conversation*)

MISS AMELIA
(*After a silence, leaning to* HENRY MACY, *saying, with great force*)

You are welcome to it. (*Pause*) You hear?

HENRY MACY

He . . . he is on parole. He is out of the penitentiary. I got this letter last week, an' he is on parole.
(*The cafe is very quiet now.* COUSIN LYMON *senses*

something *extraordinary;* HE *gets up, moves about,*
speaks to the OTHERS)

COUSIN LYMON
Who? . . . Who? . . . What?

MISS AMELIA
(Slamming her fist down on the table)
You are welcome to any letter you get from him, because
your brother is a . . . because he belong to be in that penitentiary the balance of his life!

COUSIN LYMON
Who? . . . Who is this about?

MERLIE RYAN
Marvin Macy comin' back? Is Marvin Macy . . .

MACPHAIL
Hush, you!

COUSIN LYMON (To HENRY MACY)
You got a brother? Hunh? What is all this?

MISS AMELIA
Marvin Macy belong to be in that penitentiary the balance
of his life!

COUSIN LYMON
(Beside himself with curiosity and a strange excite-
ment)
WHO IS MARVIN MACY? Parole? What . . . what did he do?

MISS AMELIA
(Still to HENRY MACY)
You hear me?

COUSIN LYMON
(To STUMPY MACPHAIL*)*

What did he do?

MACPHAIL
(With embarrassment, not looking up)

Well, he . . . well, he robbed three filling stations . . . for
one . . .

MERLIE RYAN

Do Miss Amelia know Marvin Macy comin' back?
*(*SEVERAL *quiet him)*

HENRY MACY
(With great difficulty)

He don't say much . . . his letter don't say much . . .
'cept . . .

*(*HE *stops)*

MISS AMELIA *(Her fists clenched)*

. . . 'Cept?

(Dead silence)

HENRY MACY *(Finally)*

'Cept he is comin' back here.
(Flurry of excitement)

MISS AMELIA
(A commandment)

He will never set his split hoof on my premises! Never. That
is all!

(Swings around to the OTHERS*)*
Get back to your drinkin', all of you!
*(Self-conscious and half-hearted return to normalcy.
But* COUSIN LYMON *will not be put by)*

COUSIN LYMON
(Turning to FIRST TOWNSMAN*)*
Tell me about Marvin Macy; tell me what he done!

FIRST TOWNSMAN *(Moving away)*
Let it be.

COUSIN LYMON
Who is Marvin Macy?

SECOND TOWNSMAN
Go on about your business, now.

COUSIN LYMON
(To no one; to the center of the room)
Who is . . . who is . . .
(Sees MISS AMELIA *moving to the porch; runs after
her)*
Who is he? Amelia, who is Marvin Macy?

MISS AMELIA
(Going on to the porch)
Finish your dinner.

COUSIN LYMON
(Following her on to the porch)
Amelia, who is Marvin Macy? I want to know who this man
is! Who is . . . ?
*(*MISS AMELIA *and* COUSIN LYMON *see* MARVIN MACY
simultaneously. Tense silence)

MISS AMELIA
(As COUSIN LYMON *takes a couple of tentative steps
toward* MARVIN MACY, *stops)*
You clear outa here! You get on!
(Silence for a second, then MARVIN MACY *laughs,*

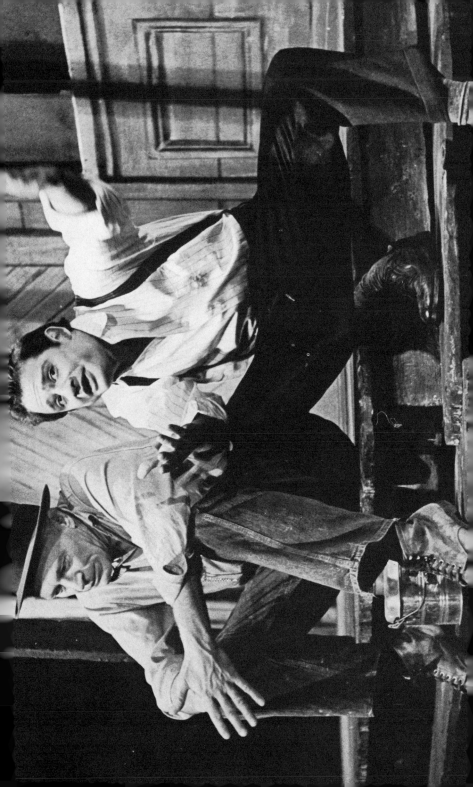

turns, exits. MISS AMELIA *stares after him, turns to
go in, goes, leaving* COUSIN LYMON *alone on the
porch)*

COUSIN LYMON *(Alone)*

WHO IS MARVIN MACY?

(Stays where HE *is)*

THE NARRATOR

Who is Marvin Macy? Who is Marvin Macy? Now, while
no one would tell Cousin Lymon about Marvin Macy
that night in the cafe . . . *(Lighting shift to day here)*
. . . people are braver in the daylight, and the next day it
was not hard at all for him to learn what he wanted to know.
And what he found out was this . . . that many years ago,
back when Miss Amelia was nineteen years old, there occurred in her life a singular and awesome event: Miss Amelia
had been married. Back when Miss Amelia was nineteen years
old there were, at the same time, two brothers, the living re-
mainder of a brood of seven children. The brothers were
Marvin and Henry Macy, and Marvin was ten years younger
than his brother, Henry. And Marvin Macy was a loom-fixer
at the mill, and he was the handsomest man in the region
. . . and the wildest.

*(*COUSIN LYMON *stays on stage, way to one side.*
Music out.

MARVIN *and* HENRY MACY *come on)*

HENRY MACY

The Tanner girl . . .

MARVIN MACY

What about the Tanner girl?

HENRY MACY

She gone off to Society City.

MARVIN MACY (*Challenging*)

So?

(*No response from* HENRY)

So, let her go; she be happy there, give her some free space to run about in.

HENRY MACY

(*Sitting;* MARVIN *stays standing*)

I hear she left on account of you.

MARVIN MACY

Who says? . . . Hunh?

HENRY MACY

Mrs. Tanner. She stops me comin' back from the mill . . . yesterday . . . she say Laura go off to Society City on account of you . . .

MARVIN MACY

On account of me *what* . . . ?

HENRY MACY

Land, Marvin, *you* know.

MARVIN MACY

(*Intentionally transparent pretense of innocence*)

I don't know.

HENRY MACY

Ain't the first young girl you take out to the woods with you, ain't the first young girl you forced to leave home . . . you ruined. Ain't the first . . .

MARVIN MACY (*Bored impatience*)

I know what I *do*. (*Leers*) I know who I take walkin' in

the moonlight with me, goes out little girls comes back
women . . .

HENRY MACY

It ain't right!

MARVIN MACY *(Suddenly ugly)*

Don't you tell me what's right! God damn, for a brother you
act one hell of a lot like you was my father!

HENRY MACY
(Softer, but still to the point)

It ain't right.

MARVIN MACY

Them young girls . . . ? Them young girls you talk about
. . . *(Cruel imitation)* . . . "it ain't right" . . . *(His face
close to* HENRY's) . . . you know what they want? Hunh?
How you know what they do out there in the woods, drive
a man half out of his mind; what d' you know about that?
(Sneers) The kinda moonlight walks *you* take, Henry, them
solitary walks at night, that . . . *(Chuckles)* . . . that ain't
the same thing . . . ain't, at all. *(An afterthought; still not
kind)* 'Sides, don't think a walk in the woods with Laura
Tanner do you any harm . . . might do you some good!

HENRY MACY *(To avoid)*

She ain't the first you take out there! They ain't all pressing
theirselves up against you, free for all. They be a legal word
for what you do out there, Marvin!

MARVIN MACY *(Quietly amused)*

Yeah? What be it?

HENRY MACY

Never . . . never mind.

MARVIN MACY

They be a word for what you do out there in them woods, too, Henry.

HENRY MACY
(Embarrassed, but still brother)

You . . . you gonna get yourself in big trouble one day.

MARVIN MACY *(Sneering bravura)*

I been in trouble. Oooh, I am evil, Henry.

HENRY MACY

Carryin' marijuana around with you, and . . .

MARVIN MACY
(Pretending to fish into a pocket)

Want some, Henry? Want some marijuana?

HENRY MACY *(Vacant)*

It is for them who are discouraged and drawn toward death.

MARVIN MACY *(A great laugh)*

And you ain't? *(Pause)* It is also for little girls who would be women; makes their heads whirl, gives 'em that floating feelin' . . .

(Laughs again, softer)

HENRY MACY

And aside from that, all your drinkin', and you not savin' any money, an' . . .

MARVIN MACY *(Angry)*

I got steady work, an' I make good money! I spend it as I like! I don't need you tellin' me . . .

HENRY MACY (*Softly*)

All right. (*Loud*) ALL RIGHT!

MARVIN MACY (*Muttering*)

I don't need you tellin' me anything 'bout how to go about livin'. I make good money . . .

HENRY MACY (*Weary impatience*)

. . . you make good money, an' you don't need me . . . yeah, I know all about it.

MARVIN MACY

Yeah.

HENRY MACY

Yeah. Don't change nothin', though.

MARVIN MACY (*Almost whining*)

Oh, Henry.

HENRY MACY

Man like you oughta settle down, oughta get married, raise some kids.

MARVIN MACY (*Suddenly furious*)

For what! Raise kids, have 'em a life like what we had? For what!

HENRY MACY

They is no need for kids to grow up like we had to; they is . . .

(MISS AMELIA *enters, near them;* SHE *wears a dress.* SHE *looks younger—maybe her hair is down.* THEY *do not see her*)

MARVIN MACY

For what!

HENRY MACY

All right now.

MARVIN MACY

Kids better off not born!

HENRY MACY

All right.

MARVIN MACY

Damn fool idea!

MISS AMELIA *(Irony)*

Afternoon.

(HENRY MACY *rises;* MARVIN MACY *does not)*

HENRY MACY

Afternoon, Miss Amelia.

MARVIN MACY

Afternoon, Miss Amelia.

MISS AMELIA *(To* MARVIN MACY*)*

Your legs broke?

MARVIN MACY

Miss Amelia?

MISS AMELIA

I say: your legs broke?

MARVIN MACY *(Lazily)*

Why, no, Miss Amelia; my legs fine.

MISS AMELIA *(Snorts)*

I wondered. *(Purposefully, to* HENRY MACY*)* Whyn't you sit on back down, Henry?

HENRY MACY *(Resits)*

Thank you, Miss Amelia.

MARVIN MACY

Ohhhhhh.
> *(Slowly rises, mock-bows to* MISS AMELIA*)*
Half the time I forget you're a girl, Miss Amelia . . . you so big; you more like a man.

MISS AMELIA

Yeah?
> (SHE *swings backhand at* MARVIN MACY, *who ducks, laughs, sits again)*

MARVIN MACY

Temper, Miss Amelia.

MISS AMELIA *(Only half a joke)*

Don't you worry about temper. I'll knock you across the road.

MARVIN MACY

Bet you'd try.

MISS AMELIA

Bet I would. Do it, too.

MARVIN MACY

Well, you might *try*, Miss Amelia . . .

MISS AMELIA

Stand back up; I'll give you a sample.

HENRY MACY
Now, why don't you two just . . .

MISS AMELIA *(Smiling)*
Stand back up.

MARVIN MACY *(Gently)*
I don't go 'round hittin' girls, now.

MISS AMELIA
I didn't say nothin' about you hittin' me; I said I knock you across the road, an' I could do it.

MARVIN MACY *(Pleased)*
Well, maybe you could, Miss Amelia; maybe you could, at that.

MISS AMELIA
'Course, you could always pull a razor on me, like I hear you done to that man over in Cheehaw you fought.

MARVIN MACY *(Mock shock)*
Miss Amelia!

MISS AMELIA
I hear about it.

MARVIN MACY
Now, what did you hear?

MISS AMELIA
I hear. I hear you take a razor to that man, an' you cut his ear off.

HENRY MACY
Oh, now.

MISS AMELIA

An' you know what else I hear?

MARVIN MACY *(Greatly amused)*

No. What else you hear?

MISS AMELIA

I hear you got that man's ear salted and dried an' you carry it around with you.

HENRY MACY *(Dogmatically)*

That ain't true.

MARVIN MACY

Now, do you think I'd do a thing like that?

HENRY MACY

That ain't *true*.

MISS AMELIA *(To HENRY MACY)*

You know? You got proof it ain't?
(To MARVIN MACY)
You got proof you ain't got that man's ear?

MARVIN MACY
(Leans back lazily)

You want proof, Miss Amelia? You wanna search me? I'll lay back real quiet and let you go through my pockets, if you have a mind to. I'll lay back real quiet.

MISS AMELIA
(Finally, after a moment's noticeable embarrassment and confusion)

Clear across the road! I'll knock you clear across the road.
(MARVIN MACY laughs; HENRY joins in)

MARVIN MACY

Uhhh-*huh!*

MISS AMELIA
*(Embarrassment back a little, begins to move to-
ward her house)*
I'll . . . I'll let you two go on back to whatever caused all
that shoutin' you two were at . . . yellin' at each other . . .

MARVIN MACY

Why, you know what we were talkin' about, Miss Amelia?
Shoutin', you say? We were talkin' about how it time for me
to get a wife, that's what.

MISS AMELIA *(Snorts)*

Who marry you?

MARVIN MACY *(Mock seriousness)*
Why, Miss Amelia, I thought you would. Don't you want to
marry me, Miss Amelia?

MISS AMELIA
(Confused for a moment, then)
In a pig's ear!
(Strides to and into her house)

MARVIN MACY
(To her retreating form)
Why, I thought you'd like that, Miss Amelia.

HENRY MACY

Bye, Miss Amelia.

MARVIN MACY

Thought you'd like that.

HENRY MACY
(*After* MISS AMELIA *has gone*)
Some jokes ain't in the best taste, Marvin.

MARVIN MACY
Hm?

HENRY MACY
Some jokes ain't in the best taste.

MARVIN MACY
(*After momentary puzzlement*)
Oh . . . no . . . that be a point, Henry . . . some jokes ain't.

HENRY MACY
No; they ain't.

MARVIN MACY
Hey, you know I be right about somethin': Miss Amelia ain't no girl; she be a woman already.

HENRY MACY
Yes, she be. Sure ain't right for you, Marvin; she be grown up.

MARVIN MACY
(*Gets up, wanders toward the door to the house*)
No. Sure ain't.

HENRY MACY
(*Gets up, prepares to leave*)
Well . . .

MARVIN MACY
Hey, Henry . . . ?

HENRY MACY

Yeah?

MARVIN MACY

A real grown-up woman.

HENRY MACY

Marvin . . .

MARVIN MACY

Hey, Henry . . . if I *was* gonna get a wife . . .

HENRY MACY

You crazy?

MARVIN MACY

Some say.

HENRY MACY

You ain't serious, Marvin. She laugh in your face.

MARVIN MACY

Hmmm? Oh, yeah, bet you right.

HENRY MACY

You ain't serious, Marvin.

MARVIN MACY
(*After a moment; smiles at* HENRY MACY)
No. I ain't serious.
(THEY *hold positions*)

THE NARRATOR

Oh, but he was; Marvin Macy was dead serious. He had, at
that moment, without knowing it, chosen Miss Amelia Evans

to be his bride. He had chosen her to be his bride, and when he realized that astonishing fact he was dismayed. For while he knew he loved her, had probably loved her for some time without knowing it, he also knew he did not deserve her. He was sick with dismay at his unworthiness. So, for two full years, Marvin Macy did not speak to Miss Amelia of his love for her, but spent that time in bettering himself in her eyes. No man in the town ever reversed his character more fully. And finally, one Sunday evening, at the end of two years, Marvin Macy returned to Miss Amelia and plighted his troth.

(MARVIN MACY *enters from stage-left, bearing a sack of chitterlins, a bunch of swamp flowers and, in the pocket of his dressy suit, a silver ring.* HE *approaches slowly, his eyes on the ground;* HE *stops a number of feet from where* MISS AMELIA *is sitting)*

MARVIN MACY
(Still not looking at her)
Evenin' Miss Amelia. *(No response)* Sure is hot.

MISS AMELIA *(After a pause)*
It so hot, what you all dressed up for a funeral for?

MARVIN MACY
(After a blushing laugh)
Oh, I . . . I am come callin'.
(Let it be understood here that there are, unless otherwise stated, varying pauses between speeches in this scene)

MISS AMELIA
Yeah? On who?

MARVIN MACY
Oh . . . on you . . . Miss Amelia.

MISS AMELIA *(Restating a fact)*
On me.

MARVIN MACY *(Laughs briefly)*
Yep . . . on you.

MISS AMELIA *(Considers it; then)*
Somethin' wrong?

MARVIN MACY
I . . .
(HE *makes a sudden decision, hurriedly brings the
bag of chitterlins and the flowers over to where*
MISS AMELIA *is, puts them on the ground below
where* SHE *is sitting, the flowers on top of the bag,
and returns to his position)*
. . . I brought you these.

MISS AMELIA *(Stares at them)*
What be these?

MARVIN MACY *(Terribly shy)*
Flowers.

MISS AMELIA
I can see that. What be in the bag?

MARVIN MACY *(As before)*
They be . . . chitterlins.

MISS AMELIA *(Mild surprise)*
Chitterlins.

MARVIN MACY
Yep.

(MISS AMELIA *descends the stairs, picks up the*
flowers as though they were a duster)

MISS AMELIA (*Reseating herself*)
What for?

MARVIN MACY
Miss Amelia?

MISS AMELIA
I say: what for? Why you bring me chitterlins and flowers?

MARVIN MACY
(*Bravely taking one or two steps forward*)
Miss Amelia, I am . . . I am a reformed person. I have
mended my ways, and . . .

MISS AMELIA
If you are come to call, sit down. Don't stand there in the
road.

MARVIN MACY
Thank . . . Thank you, Miss Amelia.
(HE *comes onto the porch and seats himself, but*
four or five feet from MISS AMELIA)
I have mended my ways; I am, like I said, a reformed person,
Miss Amelia . . .

MISS AMELIA
(*Looking at the flowers*)
What are these called?

MARVIN MACY
Hunh? . . . Oh, they . . . they be swamp flowers.

MISS AMELIA
But what are they *called?*

MARVIN MACY *(Shrugs, helplessly)*
Swamp flowers.

MISS AMELIA
They got a name.

MARVIN MACY
I . . . I don't know.

MISS AMELIA
I don't neither. *(Pause)* They got a name in some *language;* all flowers do.

MARVIN MACY
I don't know, Miss Amelia.

MISS AMELIA
I don't neither. *(Smells them)* They don't smell none.

MARVIN MACY
I'm . . . sorry.

MISS AMELIA
Don't have to smell; they pretty.

MARVIN MACY *(Blurting)*
Miss Amelia, I have mended my ways; I go to church regular, and I have . . .

MISS AMELIA
I see it. You go to church now, services an' meetings . . .

MARVIN MACY

. . . yes, an' I have learned to put money aside . . .

MISS AMELIA

. . . you have learned thrift; that good . . .

MARVIN MACY

. . . an' I have bought me some land, I have bought me ten
acres of timber over by . . .

MISS AMELIA

. . . I hear so; timber is good land . . .

MARVIN MACY

. . . an', an' I don't drink none no more . . .

MISS AMELIA

. . . don't drink? . . .

MARVIN MACY *(Blushes)*

. . . well, you know what I mean . . .

MISS AMELIA

Man don't drink none ain't natural.

MARVIN MACY

Well, I don't squander my wages away on drink an' all that
I used to . . .

MISS AMELIA

Uh-huuh.

MARVIN MACY

. . . an' . . . Miss Amelia? . . . an' I am less sportin' with
the girls now . . . I have reformed my character in that
way, too . . .

MISS AMELIA (*Nods slowly*)

I know; I hear.

MARVIN MACY

. . . an'; an' I have stopped pickin' fights with folks . . .

MISS AMELIA

You still got that ear? You still got that ear you cut off that
man in Cheehaw you fight? . . .

MARVIN MACY (*Embarrassed*)

Oh, Miss Amelia, I never done that.

MISS AMELIA (*Disbelieving*)

I *hear.*

MARVIN MACY

Oh, no, Miss Amelia, I never done that. I . . . I let that
story pass 'round . . . but I never done that.

MISS AMELIA
(*The slightest tinge of disappointment*)

Oh. That so.

MARVIN MACY

So, you see, I have reformed my character.

MISS AMELIA (*Nods*)

Would seem.

(*A long pause between them*)

MARVIN MACY

Yes.

MISS AMELIA

Land is good to have. I been dickerin' over near Society City

to pick up thirty-five acres . . . timber, too . . . man there
near broke, an' he wanna sell to me.

MARVIN MACY

Miss . . . Miss Amelia . . . *(Brings the ring from his pocket)* I brought somethin' else with me, too . . .

MISS AMELIA *(Curious)*

Yeah?

MARVIN MACY

I . . .
(Shows it to her)
. . . I brought this silver ring.

MISS AMELIA
(Looks at it; hands it back)

It silver?

MARVIN MACY

Yep, it silver. Miss Amelia, will you . . .

MISS AMELIA

Bet it cost some.

MARVIN MACY
(Determined to get it out)

Miss Amelia, will you marry me?

MISS AMELIA
*(After an interminable pause, during which she
scratches her head, then her arm, then very off-
hand)*

Sure.

MARVIN MACY
(Almost not having heard)
You . . . Yes?! . . . You will?

MISS AMELIA
(Narrowing her eyes, almost unfriendly)
I said sure.

MARVIN MACY
*(Not rising, begins sliding himself across the step
to her)*
Oh, Amelia . . .

MISS AMELIA *(Sharply)*
What?

MARVIN MACY
(In a split second studies what HE *has said wrong,
realizes it, keeps sliding)*
Oh, Miss Amelia . . .
*(*HE *reaches her, begins the gesture of putting one
arm behind her back, the other in front, prepara-
tory to kissing her.* MISS AMELIA *reacts swiftly, leans
back a bit, swings her right arm back, with a fist,
ready to hit him)*

MISS AMELIA
Whoa there, you!

MARVIN MACY
(Retreats some, slides back a few feet)
Wait 'til I tell Henry; wait 'til I tell *everybody*. *(Very hap-
py)* Oh, Miss Amelia.

MISS AMELIA *(Rises, stretches)*
Well . . . g'night.

(MARVIN MACY, *momentarily confused, but too happy to worry about it, rises, also, backs down the porch steps, begins backing off, stage left)*

MARVIN MACY

G' . . . G' . . .G'night, Miss Amelia. *(Reaches the far side of the stage, then just before turning to run off, shouts)* G'night, Miss Amelia.

(Exits)

MISS AMELIA
(Standing on the porch, alone; long pause)
G'night . . .

(Pause)

Marvin Macy.

(MISS AMELIA *goes indoors)*

NARRATOR

And the very next Sunday they were married. It was a proper church wedding, performed by the Reverend Potter, and Miss Amelia had held a bouquet of flowers, and Henry was there to give Marvin away, and it was, indeed, a proper wedding. Now it is true that some of the townspeople had misgivings about the match, but no one—not even the most evil-minded—had foreseen what was to happen: for the marriage of Marvin Macy and Miss Amelia Evans lasted only ten days . . . ten unholy days which became a legend, a whispered legend in the town.

(Interior of store visible. MISS AMELIA *and* MARVIN MACY *alone.* MISS AMELIA *wears a wedding dress, carries a wedding bouquet.* MARVIN MACY *has a flower in his coat)*

MARVIN MACY *(Shyly)*

Well, Miss Amelia . . .

MISS AMELIA
(*Picking at her dress*)

Don't know why a person's supposed to get all up in this
stuff . . . just to get married.

MARVIN MACY

I think it look . . . nice.

MISS AMELIA (*Studying the dress*)

Belong to my mother.

MARVIN MACY

It look . . . nice.

MISS AMELIA

Too short.

MARVIN MACY

It look . . . nice. You . . . you pass it on down to . . .

MISS AMELIA

Hm?

MARVIN MACY

You pass it on down to our kids . . . our daughters.

MISS AMELIA
(*Looks at him, snorts*)

Hunh! (*Laughs briefly, sardonically*) If you hungry, go eat.

MARVIN MACY

I ain't hungry, Miss Amelia.

MISS AMELIA

No? Suit yourself. I got some figgerin' to do.

MARVIN MACY *(Shyly)*

Figgerin' . . . Miss Amelia?

MISS AMELIA
(Totally oblivious of his surprise)

Yeah, I got a bargain goin' on some kindlin' I want, an' I gotta figger. I think I figgered a way to get that kindlin' good an' cheap. That farmer owe me a favor: once I fixed boils for him, an' he ain't never paid a bill he owed papa when he were alive. I kin get it good an' cheap. What you think?

MARVIN MACY

I think . . . I think it be time . . . ain't it time for bed, Miss Amelia?

MISS AMELIA

Ain't ten. You tired?

MARVIN MACY
(Sitting gently, to wait)

No. I . . . ain't tired.

MISS AMELIA

You wanna smoke a pipe? Before sleep? Ain't no pockets in this dress. Thought I had my clothes on.

MARVIN MACY

No, I don't need a pipe. Miss Amelia, it . . . time for bed.

MISS AMELIA
(Stretching; off-hand)

Yeah . . . well, c'mon . . . I'll show you where your room is.

MARVIN MACY

My . . . room . . . Miss Amelia?

MISS AMELIA
(*Going toward the stairs*)
C'mon.

MARVIN MACY (*Moving to her*)
Kin I . . . kin I take your arm?

MISS AMELIA
(*Looks at him as though* HE *were crazy. Laughs in his face*)
What for?

MARVIN MACY
Well, it is . . . proper for a groom . . . to take his bride by the hand, an' . . .

MISS AMELIA
(*Annoyed by the impracticality of his suggestion*)
I got a lamp. You want it to spill?
(MISS AMELIA, *followed by* MARVIN MACY, *climb the stairs, disappear. It becomes dark in the store, but the interior stays visible*)

THE NARRATOR
And what happened next, what happened that wedding night of Miss Amelia and Marvin Macy, no one will ever truly know. But part of it—part of it—was witnessed by Emma Hale, who had watched it, her nose pressed against the downstairs window of the store. And she could not wait to tell what she had seen.

EMMA HALE (*To* HENRY MACY)
An' it weren't no more'n a half hour after they'd gone up-stairs, him followin' after her . . .

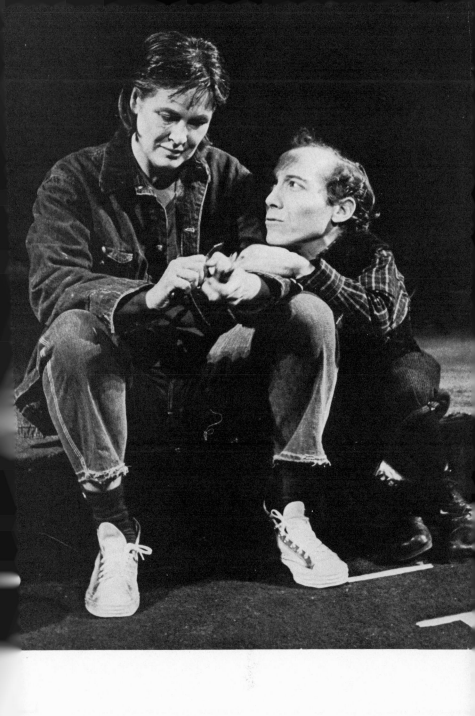

(*Pantomime from* MISS AMELIA *and* MARVIN MACY *to this*)

Miss Amelia come thumpin' back down those stairs, her face black with anger? An' she'd changed outa that dress o' hers, an' she were got up like she usually be now, an' she went into her office . . .

(*Pauses for effect*)

. . . and she stayed there 'till *dawn*. She stay there the whole night! He stayed up *there*, an' she stayed down *there*, in her office. (*Proudly*) An' how do you like that for a weddin' night?

HENRY MACY

I . . . I . . . didn't know.

EMMA HALE

All I can say is: a groom is in a sorry fix when he is unable to bring his well-beloved bride to bed with him. An' the whole town know it. There is some question there—specially a man like Marvin, his reputation: up-ending girls from here to Cheehaw an' back. Somethin' funny there.

HENRY MACY

Marvin?

MARVIN MACY
(*His attention only on* HENRY)

Henry . . . she . . .

HENRY MACY (*Gently*)

I know; I know.

MARVIN MACY (*A child*)

Henry, she don't like me . . . she don't . . . want me.

HENRY MACY

Well, now, Marvin, sometime it takes a while to . . .

MARVIN MACY

What'd I do wrong, Henry? She don't want me.

HENRY MACY (*Helplessly*)

Well, Marvin . . .

MARVIN MACY

We get upstairs, an' . . .

HENRY MACY

It take time, Marvin.

MARVIN MACY

I don't know; I don't know, Henry.

HENRY MACY (*Vaguely*)

Well . . .

MARVIN MACY
(*An idea coming to him, enthusiasm growing*)

Hey! Henry, maybe . . . maybe it 'cause I didn't give her
no . . . no weddin' gifts . . . you know, women like to have
them things. Hey, Henry? Maybe that it, huh?

HENRY MACY (*Cautious*)

Well, now . . .

MARVIN MACY

That's what I'll do, Henry: I'll go in to Society City an' . . .
an' I'll get her a bunch of stuff.

(HE *leaves the porch, heads off*)

That'll do it, Henry! I bet!

(HE *exits, happily*)

HENRY MACY *(After him)*

Maybe . . . might be.

(Stays on stage)

THE NARRATOR

And off he went to Society City, and he brought her back all kinds of things; a huge box of chocolates which cost two dollars and a half, an enamel brooch, an opal ring, and a silver bracelet which had, hanging from it, two silver lovebirds. And he gave these presents to her . . . and she put them up for sale . . . all save the chocolates . . . which she ate. And, sad to tell, these presents did not soften her heart toward him.

MISS AMELIA

Oh, by the way, I gonna drag a mattress down from upstairs; you can sleep on *it*, in front of the stove, down here in the store.

(SHE waits for some reaction, gets none, goes inside)

MARVIN MACY

(By himself; the night has deepened a little. In a soft plaintive voice)

Henry? . . . Henry?

HENRY MACY

(From far off to one side)

Yes, Marvin.

MARVIN MACY

(To the night, not to HENRY's voice)

Henry, I don't know what to do.

HENRY MACY *(Helpless, himself)*

Well, now, Marvin . . .

MARVIN MACY

I love her, Henry. I don't know what to do.

HENRY MACY

Time, Marvin. Time?

MARVIN MACY *(Pause)*

Yeah. *(Pause)* Sure, Henry.
(It comes up to daylight again now, MARVIN MACY *staying where* HE *is)*

MARVIN MACY

(Gets up, shouts at the upstairs of the house, both a threat and a promise)
I be back!

HENRY MACY

(As MARVIN MACY *passes him, exiting)*
Marvin? Marvin, where you . . .

MARVIN MACY *(Pushing past)*

I goin' into Cheehaw; I be back.
(Exits)

THE NARRATOR

There was, of course, speculation in the town on the reason Miss Amelia had married Marvin Macy in the first place. No one doubted that *he* loved *her*, but as to why she had accepted his proposal in the first place there were myriad opinions. And while some people were . . . confused by the course of events, no one could honestly say he was surprised.

MARVIN MACY
(Reenters, moves inside to MISS AMELIA; SHE *looks
up at him with a cool curiosity)*
Miss Amelia?

MISS AMELIA
You doin' a lot of travelin', I notice.

MARVIN MACY
I . . . I been to Cheehaw today.

MISS AMELIA *(Indifferent)*
Yeah? What you do there?

MARVIN MACY
I went into Cheehaw, an' . . . an' I saw a lawyer.

MISS AMELIA
(Suddenly on her guard)
Yeah? What you seein' a lawyer about?

MARVIN MACY *(Shy; embarrassed)*
Well, now . . .

MISS AMELIA *(Smelling trouble)*
What you know about lawyers?

MARVIN MACY
Well, I got me a lawyer . . . *(Takes out the paper)* . . . an'
I got this paper drawn up . . .

MISS AMELIA *(Belligerently)*
Yeah, an'? . . .

MARVIN MACY
(*Shy, but enthusiastic*)

An' what I done, I got this paper drawn up, an' I had the
deed to my timber land . . . the . . . the ten acres of timber
land I bought with my savin's the past couple years . . . an'
I had the deed to my timber land turned over to you, Miss
Amelia. I had it put in your name; it all yours.

(HE *eagerly holds the paper out to* MISS AMELIA)

MISS AMELIA
(SHE *looks at him for a moment, no expression on
her face, then* SHE *takes the paper from him, not
snatching it, but not taking a gift, either.* SHE *studies it*)

Hm!

MARVIN MACY

It all legal, Miss Amelia; I seen to that.

MISS AMELIA (*Still studying it*)

Hm.

MARVIN MACY

Them ten acres all yours now.

MISS AMELIA (*Still studying*)

Unh-hunh.

MARVIN MACY (*Shy*)

I . . . I thought you'd be pleased . . . Miss Amelia.

MISS AMELIA
(*Folding the paper, putting it in her jeans, rising*)

Yeah; it all legal.

MARVIN MACY

It is everything I have in the world.

MISS AMELIA
(Moving toward the door)

It legal.

MARVIN MACY

It is everything I have in the world, an' . . . I thought it would please you to have it.

MISS AMELIA

It adjoin *my* timber land, *my* acres; it make a nice spread.

MARVIN MACY *(Bewildered)*

Miss Amelia . . .

MISS AMELIA *(Daring him)*

Yeah?

MARVIN MACY
(His eyes on his feet)

I am not . . . as comfortable as I might be, sleepin' down in the store, in front of the stove, like I am.

MISS AMELIA *(No compassion)*

Oh no?

MARVIN MACY

No, I am not too comfortable sleepin' there.
(There is a pleading in this)

MISS AMELIA *(Considers it)*

Oh. *(Then)* Well, in that case then, why don't you pull your

mattress out onto the porch, sleep there, or move over into
the smoke house? Plenty of places you can sleep.
      (SHE *waits, challengingly, for his reply*)

MARVIN MACY
(Too pitiable to be pitied)
I'd . . . you know where I'd rather sleep, Miss Amelia.

MISS AMELIA
Or why don't you just move back with your brother Henry?
      (SHE *turns, goes indoors*)

MARVIN MACY
*(Sits for a moment, contemplates his hopelessness;
speaks to himself, gathering resolve)*
I am your husband; you are married to me, Miss Amelia
Evans.
      (HE *gets up, follows her into the store, says to her
with firmness and bravura*)
Where is your likker?

MISS AMELIA *(Preoccupied)*
Hm?

MARVIN MACY
Gimme some likker!

MISS AMELIA
(With some distaste)
You takin' up drinkin' again? High noon drinkin'?

MARVIN MACY
Gimme some likker!

MISS AMELIA
(Her eyes narrowing)
You want some likker, you get your money up like anybody
else.

MARVIN MACY
(Digging into his pocket)
I got my money; you give me that likker!
(HE slams the money down on the counter)
*(SHE reaches under the counter, brings up a bottle
and slams it down on the counter. The two glower
at each other)*
(Murderously)
Thank you.

MISS AMELIA *(The same)*
You welcome.

MARVIN MACY
(Taking the bottle)
Now, I think I'll just take me off into the swamp an' have
me a few drinks, an' then I think I'll just come back here
an' . . .

MISS AMELIA
You get yourself full of likker you don't set your foot in my
house!

MARVIN MACY
We see about that . . . Mrs. Macy!

MISS AMELIA *(A threat)*
You come back here drunk you wish you never born.

MARVIN MACY
We see about that! I love you, Miss Amelia.

MISS AMELIA

OUTA HERE!!

MARVIN MACY
(Still coming toward her)
You my bride, an' I gonna make you my wife.

MISS AMELIA
(Her fist cocked)
One step more, you!

MARVIN MACY
(At her now, tries to embrace her)
I love you, Miss Amelia.
(At this, MISS AMELIA swings at him, cracks him right in the jaw, with such force that HE staggers back and crashes, hard, against a wall; slumps there a little, one hand to his mouth)

MISS AMELIA
(Her fists still cocked)
OUT! OUT!

MARVIN MACY
(Surprised and hurt)
You . . . you broke my tooth; you . . . you broke one of my teeth.

MISS AMELIA
(Beginning to advance on him)
I break your head you don't get outa here!

MARVIN MACY
(Scrambling to get out, keeping as far from her advancing form as HE can)
You . . . you broke my tooth.

MISS AMELIA *(Advancing)*

OUT!

MARVIN MACY
(Backs out onto the porch, down the steps)
You . . . you hit me.

MISS AMELIA
(Towering above him)
You stay out, an' don't you never come back!

MARVIN MACY
(Still unable to believe it)
You hit me.

MISS AMELIA

You hear me? Don't you never come back! (MISS AMELIA *goes back into the store)*
　　(MARVIN MACY *gets up, moves front and center, broods at the footlights.)*
　　(HE *reconsiders, marches up the steps, pauses momentarily, then, with renewed resolve, gets to the door. Forcefully:)*
Miss Amelia?
　　(SHE *turns around where* SHE *is, behind the counter, perhaps, looks at him)*
Miss Amelia, I comin' back in.
　　　　(SHE *moves to another area of the store)*
You hear me? I got rights to be in here, as you is my wife an' what's yours is mine, too. So, I comin' in!
　　(MISS AMELIA *picks up her shotgun, breaks it, reaches for shells, loads it, begins to walk toward* MARVIN MACY)
I got my rights now, an' I'm comin' in there, an' I'm gonna . . . (HE *sees the gun in her hand)*

(SHE *keeps advancing, pointing the gun at him,
holding it at hip level*)

You . . . you can't do that, now . . . you . . .

(HE *retreats from the door, as* MISS AMELIA *keeps advancing*)

I got my rights, an' . . .

(HE *backs down the steps as* MISS AMELIA *comes out
on the porch, stony-faced, the shotgun still pointed
at him*)

You . . . you keep that thing off me!

(HE *keeps backing off, finally stops*)

Miss Amelia . . .

(*So plaintively*)

I love you.

MISS AMELIA

(*Sits on the porch, the gun is still on him*)

You come one step closer, I blast your head off. You step one
foot on my property again, I shoot you.

MARVIN MACY

(*Stands stock still for a moment, then breaks, moves
off past* HENRY MACY)

I'm leavin', Henry, I can't take no more; I can't take no more
of this, Henry.

(*Exits*)

HENRY MACY

(*Moving to where* MISS AMELIA *is*)

Miss . . . Miss Amelia?

MISS AMELIA

(*In a rage, but abstracted*)

Yeah? Whadda ya want?

HENRY MACY

Miss Amelia, Marvin say he leavin'.
(SHE *does not react*)
He say he gonna take off from you.

MISS AMELIA
(Finally)
What this I hear 'bout a bridge gonna be built . . . ten mile up, or so. What about that? I hear they gonna have prison labor put it up. Gonna have the chain gang work on it.

HENRY MACY

He say he gonna . . . leave town.

MISS AMELIA

Been thinkin' . . . been thinkin' of havin' the prison farm bring some trusties work my cotton. It cheap labor.

HENRY MACY

I . . . You could do that, Miss Amelia.

MISS AMELIA
(Belligerently, almost a dare)
I know I could.

HENRY MACY

I . . .
(Decides to say nothing, moves away)
Well . . .
(Touches two fingers to his forehead)
Miss Amelia.

MISS AMELIA

Henry.
(Dusk begins to fall now. MISS AMELIA *stays sitting on her porch, the gun across her knees.* MARVIN

MACY *comes back on stage, carrying his tin suitcase.*
NOTE: *While it is true that on stage the* MACY
BROTHERS *and* MISS AMELIA *will be in fairly close
proximity, the following scene must give the im-
pression that* MISS AMELIA *cannot overhear what is
being said)*

MARVIN MACY *(Quietly)*

I'm leavin', Henry.

HENRY MACY

Are you, Marvin?

MARVIN MACY

Yep.

(Almost tearful)

I can't take no more.

HENRY MACY

No. I don't figger so.

MARVIN MACY

So I'm takin' off.

HENRY MACY

Where you goin', Marvin?

MARVIN MACY

I don't *know.* I go somewhere; I get away from *here.*

HENRY MACY

It best . . . I suppose.

MARVIN MACY

You write me a letter?

HENRY MACY

Why, sure I write you, Marvin, you tell me where you are . . .

MARVIN MACY

No. I don't mean that.
(Takes paper and a pencil from his pocket)
You write a letter *for* me, you put down what I tell you.

HENRY MACY

Oh!
(Takes the paper and pencil from MARVIN MACY,
takes the tin suitcase to use as a writing table)
All right, Marvin; I ready.

MARVIN MACY

You take down just what I tell you.

HENRY MACY *(Quietly, patiently)*

Yes, Marvin.

MARVIN MACY
*(*HENRY MACY *always writing)*
Dear Miss Amelia, my wife. Underline wife.

HENRY MACY

Yes, Marvin.

MARVIN MACY

Dear Miss Amelia, my *wife.* I hate you.

HENRY MACY

Marvin . . .

MARVIN MACY

Put it down! I hate you. I love you.

HENRY MACY

Marvin . . .

MARVIN MACY

Do what I tell you! I love you. I have loved you for two
years, an' I have reformed my ways to be worthy of you. I
hate you. You gettin' all this?

HENRY MACY

Yes, Marvin.

MARVIN MACY

I . . . I hate you with all the power of my love for you. I
woulda been a good husband to you, an' I loved you for two
years 'fore I even dared speak my love for you, you . . . you
no-good rotten . . .

HENRY MACY

Slow down, Marvin . . . you no-good rotten . . .

MARVIN MACY

. . . you no-good rotten cross-eyed ugly lump!

HENRY MACY

Miss Amelia's eyes don't cross . . .

MARVIN MACY

When she mad! When she mad one eye bang right into her
nose. Yes.

HENRY MACY

I . . . I never noticed.

MARVIN MACY

I . . . I reformed my character, an' I made myself worthy of
you, an' the night you said yes you marry me no man ever

been happier . . . ever. I gonna come back some day an' kill
you!

HENRY MACY

Marvin, you don't mean that, now . . .

MARVIN MACY

You put it down! I gonna come back some day an' kill you.
I gonna . . . I gonna bust your face open, I gonna . . . I
gonna tear your arms outa your body like they bug wings.

HENRY MACY

Slow down, now.

MARVIN MACY

Write fast!

HENRY MACY

I writin' fast. You want it readable, don't you?

MARVIN MACY

Yes. No. I don't care.

HENRY MACY

I doin' the best I can.

MARVIN MACY

I . . . I give you my land, land I worked hard for, 'cause I
thought it'd please you; I . . . I bought you jewels, I bought
you jewelry, an' you put it up for *sale*. You treated me like
nothin', an' I *loved* you. I . . . I love you, Miss Amelia; I
love you. An' . . .

HENRY MACY
(As MARVIN MACY *pauses*)

Go on, Marvin.

MARVIN MACY *(Almost tearfully)*

An' I goin' away now, I goin' away an' I never comin' back *(A rush)* An' when I come back I gonna fix you, I gonna kill you!

HENRY MACY
(As MARVIN MACY pauses again)

Yeah?

MARVIN MACY
(In a sort of disgusted, sad rush)

With all my love very truly yours your husband Marvin Macy.

HENRY MACY *(As HE finishes)*

You . . . you wanna sign it?

MARVIN MACY

No, you write my name down, but I gonna sign it special.
  (HE takes out his knife and gingerly jabs his thumb, drawing blood)
Here, gimme that.
  (HE bends down, bloods the bottom of the letter with his thumb)
That make it all official.

HENRY MACY

You . . . you want me give her this?

MARVIN MACY

After I go; I goin' now.
  (HE picks up his tin suitcase)

HENRY MACY *(Gets up)*

I take care of it.

MARVIN MACY
(Almost not wanting to go)
Well, Henry . . .

HENRY MACY
Marvin, you take care now.

MARVIN MACY
I'll . . . *(Shrugs)* take care of myself.

HENRY MACY
Don't go . . . gettin' in any trouble.

MARVIN MACY
(A brief, rueful laugh)
You know, Henry? I wouldn't be surprised one bit if I did?
Wouldn't surprise me I turned into one of the worst people
you ever saw?

HENRY MACY
You . . . stay good now.

MARVIN MACY
(A sudden, sick violence)
WHY?

HENRY MACY
You . . . you take care.

MARVIN MACY
Well . . . *(Pause)* . . . Goodbye, Henry.

HENRY MACY
(As MARVIN MACY exits)
Goodbye . . . Marvin.

(HENRY MACY *watches after* MARVIN MACY *for a moment, looks at the letter in his hand, turns, slowly walks to the foot of the steps, where* MISS AMELIA *is sitting*)

HENRY MACY (*Quietly*)

Miss Amelia.

MISS AMELIA

That loom-fixer take off? Your brother finally clear out?

HENRY MACY (*As before*)

Yeah. He gone.

MISS AMELIA
(*After a brief silence*)

Good riddance.

HENRY MACY

He . . .

(*Hands her the letter*)

. . . He want you to have this.

MISS AMELIA
(*Glances at it only long enough to realize it is a letter*)

Good riddance.

HENRY MACY

Well . . . 'night, Miss Amelia.

MISS AMELIA (*Pause*)

'Night, Henry.

(HENRY MACY *exits,* MISS AMELIA, *left alone on stage, begins to read the letter.*
(*Music up, if not used throughout so far*)

THE NARRATOR

And so ended the ten days of marriage of Miss Amelia Evans and Marvin Macy and answers the question that Cousin Lymon asked some years later. Who is Marvin Macy? Who is Marvin Macy?

MISS AMELIA *and* COUSIN LYMON *alone on the porch.*

COUSIN LYMON

Amelia!

MISS AMELIA

Yeah?

COUSIN LYMON

I been learnin' some things, Amelia.

MISS AMELIA

Yeah? What?

COUSIN LYMON
(*After a long pause; quietly, seriously, with no trace of sport in it*)
Amelia? Why you never tell me you married?
(*This startles* MISS AMELIA; *maybe she rises, walks a few steps, kicks a post, does not look at* COUSIN LYMON)

MISS AMELIA
(*Finally; hoarsely, angrily*)

I ain't!

COUSIN LYMON
(Quietly, persistently)
Yes, you be. You married Marvin Macy, years an' years ago.
You married.

MISS AMELIA *(A pretense)*
No!

COUSIN LYMON
Why you never tell me that?

MISS AMELIA
(Convincing herself)
I ain't married!

COUSIN LYMON
Why you never tell me you married, Amelia?

MISS AMELIA
(Finally turning, facing him)
I *were* married. I were married, to that no-account loom-fixer
. . . but that is past . . . over! . . . done!

COUSIN LYMON
(The same quiet insistence)
You ever divorce from him?

MISS AMELIA
He run off; he run off years ago; I ain't married to him no
more!

COUSIN LYMON
You ever divorce from him?

MISS AMELIA *(Furious)*
HE RUN OFF!! *(Then, finally, softer)* I ain't married no more.

COUSIN LYMON
(Quietly, logically)
Oh, yes you be. You still married to him. Why you never tell
me about that, Amelia?

MISS AMELIA
(Returning to him, sitting, quieter)
It . . . it long ago; it . . . it way in the past.
(As COUSIN LYMON *just looks at her)*
It . . . It don't have nothin' to do with . . . nothin'.

COUSIN LYMON
I find it mighty strange you never tell me about that, Amelia.

MISS AMELIA
(Strangely shy)
Ain't . . . weren't nothin' to tell. I . . . I married him . . .
he run off. *(Almost pleading)* He . . . he no good, Cousin
Lymon. He never were a good man.

COUSIN LYMON
You married him.

MISS AMELIA *(Shyer yet)*
We were . . . we never really . . . *married.*

COUSIN LYMON
You promise you never have secrets from me, Amelia. Give
me a real funny feelin', . . . knowin' you keep things from
me; give me a feelin' I don't like.

MISS AMELIA
It weren't no real secret, Cousin Lymon. I don't . . . I don't
like you to worry none about things; I like you to be comfortable, an' . . . an' happy.

COUSIN LYMON

It give me a feelin' I don't like.

MISS AMELIA

It were nothin' for you to know.

COUSIN LYMON

(Turning on her; almost savage; yes, savage)
It were nothin' for me to *know!?!*

MISS AMELIA

I . . . I don't keep much from you, Cousin Lymon; you
know my business, my . . . my accounts; I told you all
about my poppa, an' all . . .

COUSIN LYMON *(Accusing)*

All 'cept Marvin Macy.

MISS AMELIA *(Acquiescing)*

All 'cept Marvin Macy.

COUSIN LYMON

(A change begins to come over him; HE *is through
chastising* MISS AMELIA: *an excitement has come
into his voice)*
An' Marvin Macy, he . . . he is, what I hear tell, such a
man!

MISS AMELIA

(Still wrapped in thought)
Huuh! A no good.

COUSIN LYMON

You . . . you keep from me the most . . . the most excitin'
thing in your life.

MISS AMELIA *(Still half-hearing)*

Never been no good, that one.

COUSIN LYMON

An' you keep the fact of him from me, the most important fact of all in your whole life . . .

MISS AMELIA
(Becoming aware of what HE *is saying)*

Cousin Lymon . . . ?

COUSIN LYMON
(Caught up with it now)

. . . a man like Marvin Macy, who has been *everywhere,* who has seen things no other man never seen, who . . .

MISS AMELIA *(Disbelief)*

Cousin Lymon!

(Music begins here)

COUSIN LYMON

. . . who has . . . who has *(Wonder comes into his voice)* been to *Atlanta!*

MISS AMELIA
(Trying to gather what is going on)

Atlanta ain't much.

COUSIN LYMON

Who has been to *Atlanta,* an' . . . *(Religious awe enters his voice now)* an' who has had to do with the *law* . . . an' *(This is the ecstasy)* who has spent time in the *penitentiary.* Oh, Amelia! You have kept this from me!

MISS AMELIA
(*Anger coming through*)
He is a common criminal, that's all!

COUSIN LYMON
Oh, Amelia, he has been in the penitentiary, an' . . . an' I
bet he spent time on the chain gang. Oh, Amelia!

MISS AMELIA (*Confused*)
You . . . you seen the chain gang, Cousin Lymon.

COUSIN LYMON
Yes!

MISS AMELIA
A bunch of common criminals, chained together by the an-
kle, workin' on the roads in the broilin' sun, a guard standin'
over 'em with a gun.

COUSIN LYMON
Yes! Yes! Yes! Amelia!

MISS AMELIA (*Pleading*)
Cousin Lymon . . . they common criminals, they . . . they
got no freedom.

COUSIN LYMON
I know, Amelia . . . but they *together.*

MISS AMELIA
(*After a long pause; shyly*)
We together . . . Cousin Lymon.

COUSIN LYMON (*Dismissing it*)
Yes, Amelia, we together.

MISS AMELIA

An' . . . an' we got a good life together.

COUSIN LYMON *(Same)*

Oh, yes, of course, Amelia. *(The ecstasy returns)* An' they are together, those men, an' . . . an' how they *sing*, Amelia! You hear them sing, Amelia?

MISS AMELIA

(Retreating into her mind)

Yes, I hear them sing.

COUSIN LYMON

An' . . . an' they . . . *together.*
(Silence.
Music stops abruptly. MARVIN MACY *enters from stage-left, stays there, leans against the proscenium, maybe, whittling on a piece of wood.* MISS AMELIA *and* COUSIN LYMON *see him simultaneously.* MISS AMELIA *rises, stiffens, her fists clenched.* MARVIN MACY *stays lounging.* COUSIN LYMON *gets up, moves slowly, cautiously toward* MARVIN MACY)

MISS AMELIA *(To* MARVIN MACY)

You clear outa here!
*(*COUSIN LYMON *continues his slow move toward* MARVIN MACY)

MARVIN MACY

(Throws his head back, laughs contemptuously at MISS AMELIA. COUSIN LYMON *continues moving toward him, is quite near him now.*
To COUSIN LYMON, *contemptuously)*
Whatta you want, bug?

MISS AMELIA

Cousin Lymon!

COUSIN LYMON *(Waving her off)*

Leave it be, Amelia.

(Approaches MARVIN MACY*)*

You . . . you be Marvin Macy.

(With this, COUSIN LYMON *begins small, involuntary spasms of excitement, little jumps from the ground, strange jerks of his hands)*

You be Marvin Macy.

MARVIN MACY

(To MISS AMELIA, *but staring at* COUSIN LYMON*)*

What ails this brokeback?

MISS AMELIA *(Not moving)*

You clear out!

COUSIN LYMON

(His spasms continuing)

You been . . . you been to Atlanta, an' . . . an' . . . an' . . .

MARVIN MACY

Is the runt throwin' a fit?

COUSIN LYMON *(As before)*

An' . . . an' . . . an' you been to the penitentiary?

*(*MARVIN MACY *backhands* COUSIN LYMON *a sharp cuff on the ear which sends him sprawling backwards toward center-stage.* HE *falls, scrambles up)*

MARVIN MACY

That'll learn you, brokeback, starin' at me!

COUSIN LYMON

(On his feet, staring at MARVIN MACY, *but with a hand stopping signal to* MISS AMELIA *who has taken a step down the porch steps)*

Leave it be, Miss Amelia . . . just . . . leave . . . it . . . be . . .

MISS AMELIA

I'll fix that no-good!

COUSIN LYMON

(His eyes firmly on MARVIN MACY: *a command to* MISS AMELIA)

Leave me alone, Amelia! Just leave it be!

MISS AMELIA *(A hopeless call)*

Cousin Lymon!

COUSIN LYMON

Leave off, Amelia; leave off.

MARVIN MACY *(Laughs, turns)*

Bye . . . Mrs. Macy.

(Exits)

COUSIN LYMON

Marvin Macy!

MISS AMELIA

(As COUSIN LYMON *follows* MARVIN MACY *off-stage)*

Cousin Lymon?

COUSIN LYMON *(From off-stage)*

Marvin Macy! Marvin Macy! Marvin Macy!

*(*MISS AMELIA *is left alone on stage in the deepening night . . .*

Music holds)

Music begins.
Tableau: MISS AMELIA *on the porch, one step down.*

THE NARRATOR

The time has come to speak about love. Now consider three
people who were subject to that condition. Miss Amelia,
Cousin Lymon, and Marvin Macy.

But what sort of thing is love? First of all, it is a joint experience between two persons, but that fact does not mean
that it is a similar experience to the two people involved.
There are the lover and the beloved, but these two come
from different countries. Often the beloved is only the stimulus for all the stored-up love which has lain quiet within the
lover for a long time hitherto. And somehow every lover
knows this. He feels in his soul that his love is a solitary
thing. He comes to know a new, strange loneliness.

Now, the beloved can also be of any description: the most
outlandish people can be the stimulus for love. Yes, and the
lover may see this as clearly as anyone else—but that does
not affect the evolution of his love one whit. Therefore, the
quality and value of any love is determined solely by the
lover himself.

It is for this reason that most of us would rather love than
be loved; and the curt truth is that, in a deep secret way, the
state of being beloved is intolerable to many; for the lover
craves any possible relation with the beloved, even if this
experience can cause them both only pain.

But though the outward facts of love are often sad and ridic-
ulous, it must be remembered that no one can know what
really takes place in the soul of the lover himself. So, who
but God can be the final judge of any love? But one thing
can be said about these three people—all of whom, Miss
Amelia, Cousin Lymon, and Marvin Macy, all of whom were
subject to the condition of love. The thing that can be said
is this: No good will come of it.

Music still holding.

MISS AMELIA *rises right at the end of* THE NARRATOR'S *speech, goes indoors, leaving the stage momentarily empty. It is still evening*

Music out; MISS AMELIA *has gone inside.* MARVIN MACY *and* HENRY MACY *come on stage together, with* COUSIN LYMON *trailing after them, peripheral, but hovering*

MARVIN MACY
(To COUSIN LYMON: *ugly)*
You quit followin' me!? You hear!?

HENRY MACY
Oh, let him be. He don't do no harm.

MARVIN MACY *(To* HENRY MACY)
Followin' me around like some damn dog . . . yippin' at my heels. *(Falsetto)* "Marvin Macy; hello there, Marvin Macy; Marvin Macy, Marvin Macy." *(Natural voice again)* Drive a man crazy.
(Back to COUSIN LYMON)
Whyn't you get on back to your friend . . . jabber at her?

COUSIN LYMON
(Shy, but almost flirtatious)
Oh, now, I ain't no trouble.

HENRY MACY
Marvin, he don't do no harm.

MARVIN MACY
Damn brokeback, trailin' after me.
(To COUSIN LYMON, *loud)*
What you want, anyway!?

COUSIN LYMON (*Shy*)
Oh . . . I, I don't want nothin'.

MARVIN MACY (*To himself*)
Damn bug.

HENRY MACY
You . . . you passin' through, Marvin? You on your way
somewhere?

MARVIN MACY
(*With a mean grin*)
Oh, I don't know, Henry; don't got no plans. I, uh . . . I
might settle a spell.

HENRY MACY (*Sorry*)
Oh, I thought you might be on your way through.

MARVIN MACY (*Ugly*)
Whatsa matter, Henry, don't you want me 'round here?

COUSIN LYMON
Stay, Marvin Macy. Don't go on nowhere.

MARVIN MACY (*To* COUSIN LYMON)
You shut up, you damn little . . .
(*Switches his attention to* HENRY MACY)
You see? You see? That brokeback want me to stay. Whatsa
matter with you, Henry? Why you so eager to have me move
on?

HENRY MACY (*Hesitant*)
It just . . . it just that things all settled down now, now you
been gone so long, an' . . . I figgered you might be plannin'
to stir up . . . you know . . . some trouble.

MARVIN MACY
(After a great laugh)
Me? Stir up trouble? Why, whatever could you mean?
(COUSIN LYMON *giggles in support of* MARVIN MACY)
Look you!
(This to COUSIN LYMON*)*
You been followin' me around near a week now, wigglin'
your ears at me, flappin' around, dancin' . . . you don't
go home 'cept for your eats an' bed. What you expectin' me
to do . . . *adopt* you?

COUSIN LYMON
(With exaggerated longing)
Oh, Marvin Macy . . . *would* you? Would you do that?

MARVIN MACY
(Takes a swipe at him which COUSIN LYMON *ducks
expertly, laughs)*
Damn little lap dog.
(But there is kindness in the contempt)

HENRY MACY
An' . . . an' I hoped you wasn't plannin' to stir up no trouble.

MARVIN MACY
Maybe just you tired of havin' me move in on you. That
house of yours half mine, just like this place here, half mine
you know, but I 'spect you got so used to livin' there all by
yourself you got a little selfish in your middle-age.

HENRY MACY *(Quietly)*
You welcome to stay long as you like.

MARVIN MACY *(Unrelenting)*
Or maybe you don't want no ex-convict hangin' around you.

Well, I tell you somethin', Henry: I ain't quite sure why I
come back, not that there ain't no scores to settle, but I ain't
quite sure *why* I come back; just thought I'd have a look
around.

HENRY MACY

Miss Amelia is . . .

MARVIN MACY *(Suddenly harsh)*

Who said anythin' bout *her?* Hunh? I bring her up?

HENRY MACY

Miss Amelia is . . . settled down, now; she is . . . she have
Cousin Lymon with her.
                    (Cousin LYMON *giggles)*
. . . an' she got her cafe, an' . . . an' everythin' is quiet an'
settled.

MARVIN MACY

Yeah, she got quite a business goin' for herself, hunh? She
takin' in good money, I bet, hunh?

HENRY MACY *(Defensively)*

Miss Amelia run the cafe for . . . us, for all of *us:* it be . . .
it be a good place to come. It be a special place for us. Important.

MARVIN MACY

Yeah, an' it half mine, ain't it?

HENRY MACY
(Disappointed in his brother)

Oh, Marvin!

MARVIN MACY

She still my wife; don't you forget that!

HENRY MACY

Oh, Marvin! That were years ago.

MARVIN MACY

I know how long ago it were; I had lots of time to think about it! Lots of time rottin' in that penitentiary . . . all on account of her! On account of that one!!!

HENRY MACY

That . . . that kinda thing you can't blame on no one person, Marvin.

MARVIN MACY

The hell I can't!! Who says?!

HENRY MACY *(Weakly)*

It . . . it all long past now.

MARVIN MACY

Yeah, but you got a lotta time to think on things when you in the penitentiary, Henry.
(COUSIN LYMON *giggles*)
Ain't that right, peanut?

COUSIN LYMON *(Hopefully)*

Oh, I ain't never been in the penitentiary.

MARVIN MACY *(Ironically)*

Well, maybe you will be someday, peanut.
(*Back to* HENRY MACY)
Yeah, you get a lotta time to brood on things, Henry. An' . . . you know? You start makin' *plans?* Oh, all kindsa plans.

HENRY MACY

Leave . . . leave everythin' be, Marvin. Let it all rest.

MARVIN MACY
(Concluding an interview)

Well, you just keep to your own business, Henry, an' you
let me worry on mine. All right?
(HE rises)

HENRY MACY *(Still sitting)*

You . . . you always done what you wanted, Marvin.

MARVIN MACY *(Proudly)*

Damn right, Henry; so you just let me go about my business.
(Looks at COUSIN LYMON, smiles at him)
You just let *us* go about *our* business. Right, peanut?

COUSIN LYMON *(Beside himself)*

Oh, yes, yes; oh, yes.

THE NARRATOR

It was the beginning of the destruction. And the things that
happened next were beyond imagination.

*(MARVIN MACY and COUSIN LYMON move off-stage,
COUSIN LYMON second, leaving HENRY MACY alone
on stage.*

*The interior of the cafe becomes visible; a usual
evening is in progress. Most of the TOWNSPEOPLE
are there. HENRY MACY remains stationary where HE
was, to one side of the stage. Drinking and general
conversation in the cafe, though there seems to be
a curious expectant quietness which EMMA HALE
feels SHE must comment on from time to time, by
talking too loud)*

EMMA *(Too loud)*

My, it sure is cheerful in here tonight . . . considerin' everythin'.

MACPHAIL

Oh, Emma.

EMMA *(Undaunted)*

Well, it do seem strange to me.

MISS AMELIA *(No nonsense)*

What seem strange to you, Emma?

(The group becomes quieter at this)

MRS. PETERSON

(A whispered warning)

Now, Emma, watch yourself now.

MISS AMELIA *(Louder; sterner)*

What seem strange to you, Emma?

EMMA

(Flustered at first, but regaining her composure as
SHE *goes on)*

Why, it seem strange to me that . . . uh, that everybody
sittin' here so cheerful . . .

MISS AMELIA

Why! Why that strange?

EMMA

Why . . . uh . . . *(Her eyes narrowing)* . . . it seem strange
to have everybody here save *one. (Murderously solicitous)* I
mean when poor Cousin Lymon ain't here to join in the
merriment, an' have his little supper, an' be such an enter-
*tain*ment for us all, an' to keep you *company*, Miss Amelia?
(Transparently false innocence) Where is Cousin Lymon,
Miss Amelia? Why, I hardly don't see him *ever* no more.
Where do he keep himself these days Miss Amelia?

MRS. PETERSON *(Whispered again)*
Emma!

MISS AMELIA *(Clenching her fists)*
Emma!? *(Pause as the cafe falls silent)* You shut your mouth!!

EMMA *(Feigned shock)*
But, Miss Amelia, I was just askin' to find out the where-
abouts of poor cousin . . .

MISS AMELIA
SHUT IT I SAID!!

EMMA
*(Her face back to her dinner plate, mortally of-
fended)*
Well, of course if you gonna talk *that* way I . . . I just
won't bother myself about the little runt no more, that's
all.

MISS AMELIA
Eat an' get out, Emma.

MRS. PETERSON
Oh, now, Miss Amelia, all she meant was . . .

MISS AMELIA
You, too. Both of you. Eat an' git.

EMMA *(Great dignity)*
We will do that, Miss Amelia, lest we choke to death first
on whatever this is you servin'.

MISS AMELIA
Better'n your cookin'. My pigs wouldn't eat the slop you set
before yourself in your own kitchen.

MACPHAIL
(A little drunk; genial)
Ladies. Now, *please.*

MISS AMELIA *(Grumpily)*
She can't talk that way about the food in this cafe.
(HENRY MACY enters)
Evenin', Henry.

HENRY MACY
*(As several say evening to him, chooses his solitary
table)*
Evenin', Miss Amelia.

MISS AMELIA
*(Comes up to him, tries to take care none of the
others overhear)*
You, uh . . . have you, uh . . . seen Cousin Lymon?

HENRY MACY
(Not looking at her)
Yeah, I have, Miss Amelia. He with Marvin. He with Mar-
vin again.

MISS AMELIA *(After a pause)*
Eats, or likker?

HENRY MACY *(Very polite)*
I . . . I think I will just have a bottle, Miss Amelia.

MISS AMELIA *(Preoccupied)*
Suit yourself.

HENRY MACY
They not far off, I wouldn't guess; they somewhere near here
together.

MISS AMELIA
(A stab at unconcern)
Huuh; couldn't care less. Don't make no matter to me.
*(*MARVIN MACY *and* COUSIN LYMON *reappear on stage, stay lurking to one side until it is time for them to enter the cafe)*

HENRY MACY *(Embarrassed)*
I . . . I know.

EMMA *(Loud)*
What I find so remarkable is the way no one ain't allowed to talk about nothin' in this cafe, which is a public gatherin' place.

FIRST TOWNSWOMAN
(Weary of it all)
Oh, Lord.

MACPHAIL
Emma Hale, you been told to eat up an' get out.

EMMA
(With the speed of a copperhead)
Stumpy MacPhail, you go back to your boozin, an' keep outa this. *(Same loud tone)* What I find so remarkable is that now Marvin Macy back in town our little Cousin Lymon spend all his time with *him* . . . 'stead of with Miss Amelia.
(Dead silence in the cafe)

MISS AMELIA
Emma? You remember that lawyer cheated me six—seven years back? The one tried to cheat me outa some land on a deed? You remember what I did to him?

EMMA *(Pretending forgetfulness)*

Why, now . . .

MACPHAIL *(To* EMMA: *helpful)*

Why, you remember, Emma. Miss Amelia went at him, beat
him up within an inch of his life. Broke his arm? An' he
were big; an' he were a *man.*

MISS AMELIA *(To* EMMA)

Don't let it be said I wouldn't take my fists to a woman,
either . . . if she didn't keep her place.

(MARVIN MACY *and* COUSIN LYMON *start moving toward the steps,* COUSIN LYMON *leading the way)*

MERLIE RYAN *(Cheerfully)*

Miss Amelia gonna kill Emma? She gonna kill her?

SECOND TOWNSMAN

No, Merlie; 'course not.

MERLIE RYAN *(Disappointed)*

Don't see why not.

EMMA
(To MISS AMELIA; *uncertainly)*

I . . . I ain't afraid of you.

(COUSIN LYMON *and* MARVIN MACY *are up the steps
now)*

MACPHAIL *(Great slow wisdom)*

Why don't you all simmer down.

EMMA
(To MRS. PETERSON *and one of the* TOWNSWOMEN)

I ain't afraid of her.

MRS. PETERSON

You crazy if you ain't.

TOWNSWOMAN

That sure.

EMMA

I put my faith in God!

MRS. PETERSON *(Very unsure)*

Well . . . Amen.

MERLIE RYAN *(Waving a glass)*

Amen! Amen!
>   (COUSIN LYMON, *having waved* MARVIN MACY *out of
>   the light from the door, enters.* MISS AMELIA *smiles
>   to see him)*

EMMA *(Her assurance back)*

Well, here the little cockatoo now.

MACPHAIL

Evenin', Cousin Lymon.

HENRY MACY

Cousin Lymon.
>   (And, as well, a chorus of greeting. COUSIN LYMON
>   *ignores them all, marches directly up to* MISS AME-
>   LIA)

COUSIN LYMON
(Mockingly formal)

Evenin', Amelia.

MISS AMELIA

Well, where you been, Cousin Lymon; I about give you up.

COUSIN LYMON

Ooohhh . . . been about; been wanderin' around. Havin' a
little stroll an' a talk.

(*Waits very briefly to see if* MISS AMELIA *reacts to
this; she does not*)

My! Supper do smell good! What we havin'?

MISS AMELIA (*Preoccupied*)

Uh . . . what, Cousin Lymon?

COUSIN LYMON

I say: what we havin' for supper!

MISS AMELIA

Oh! Oh, well, there be ham, an' winter peas, an' hominy
grits, an' I brung out the peach preserves.

RAINEY 1 (*His mouth full*)

It be good.

RAINEY 2 (*The same*)

Yeah, it awful good.

COUSIN LYMON

Well, ain't that nice.

MISS AMELIA

You . . . you hungry now, Cousin Lymon?

COUSIN LYMON

I mean ain't that nice . . . since we have a guest for dinner
tonight.

(*The cafe becomes silent*)

I have invited a special guest for dinner tonight.

(HE *can hardly keep still waiting for* MISS AMELIA's
reaction)

MISS AMELIA
(Her reaction is slow in coming; finally, tonelessly)
Yeah?

COUSIN LYMON
Yeah.
(Calls to outside)
C'mon in, now; Miss Amelia waitin' on you.
(Absolute silence as MARVIN MACY *enters, silence
except an audible intake of breath here and there.*
MARVIN MACY *surveys the scene briefly, smiles wick-
edly at* MISS AMELIA, *who is immobile, moves to an
empty table, kicks the chair out, sits down. Still
silence)*

MARVIN MACY
Hey! Brokeback! Bring me my dinner.

MERLIE RYAN
Hey, Miss Amelia; Marvin Macy back. Miss Amelia!

MACPHAIL
Shut up, you damn fool!

EMMA
(As MISS AMELIA *is still silent, immobile)*
I never thought I'd live to see it. I tell you, I never thought
I'd live to see it.

MERLIE RYAN
Miss Amelia? Marvin Macy back.
*(*RAINEY 1 *chokes on his food, has a brief choking
fit;* RAINEY 2 *slaps his back.* MISS AMELIA *doesn't
move)*

MARVIN MACY

Hey, brokeback! My dinner!

COUSIN LYMON
(*Moving to do his bidding*)

Yes; yes, Marvin.

MISS AMELIA (*Barring his way*)

Keep outa there.

COUSIN LYMON

Marvin want his dinner!

MARVIN MACY (*To* MISS AMELIA)

Let him through!!

MISS AMELIA
(*Advancing on* MARVIN MACY)

Look you!

MARVIN MACY

Yeah?
(THEY *face each other,* MARVIN MACY *having risen; perhaps his chair has fallen over.* THEY *both clench their fists, but near their sides; they begin to circle each other. The tension is immense*)

COUSIN LYMON
(*From behind the counter*)

You like grits, Marvin?

MARVIN MACY
(*His eyes never off* MISS AMELIA)

Pile 'em on.

MISS AMELIA
(To COUSIN LYMON, *her eyes never off* MARVIN
MACY)
There some rat poison under the counter while you at it;
put a little on for flavor.

MRS. PETERSON
I gonna faint.

EMMA
Hush!

MARVIN MACY
(As THEY *continue circling each other)*
I found that trap you set for me in the woods where I hunt.
That woulda killed me good, wouldn't it?

MISS AMELIA
It woulda done the job.

MARVIN MACY *(Murderously)*
You watch yourself.

COUSIN LYMON
(Appearing with a heaping plate)
Dinner! Dinner!
*(*MISS AMELIA *suddenly swings around and stalks out
of the cafe to the porch steps, sits. Action continues inside, though maybe the interior lights dim a
little; certainly the interior conversation, such as it
is, lessens in volume.* HENRY MACY *waits a moment,
then follows* MISS AMELIA *out on to the porch)*

HENRY MACY
Miss Amelia? *(No reply)* Miss Amelia?

MISS AMELIA *(Finally)*

Leave me be.

HENRY MACY

He . . . he gonna move on soon. I know it.

MISS AMELIA *(Doubting)*

Yeah?

HENRY MACY *(Soothing)*

Sure, he move on; ain't no place for him here.

MISS AMELIA *(With deepest irony)*

You sure, huuh?

HENRY MACY *(Unsure)*

Sure.

(Music up.

During THE NARRATOR'S *speech,* MISS AMELIA *and* HENRY MACY *return inside the cafe, where life goes on,* COUSIN LYMON *waiting on* MARVIN MACY, MISS AMELIA *staying off to one side. Maybe there is barely audible conversation under this speech)*

THE NARRATOR

Oh, but Henry Macy was wrong, for Marvin did not move on. He stayed in the town, and every night the cafe was open he would arrive for dinner, and Cousin Lymon would wait on him, and bring him liquor for which he never paid a cent. And during these nights, which stretched into weeks, Miss Amelia did nothing. She did nothing at all, except to stand to one side and watch.

(Appropriate action for the following)

But every night one thing would be sure to happen. Once every night, sometimes for no reason at all that anyone could see, Miss Amelia and Marvin Macy would approach each

other, their fists clenched, and they would circle one another, and it was during these rituals that the townspeople
expected blows to be struck . . . but it never happened.

All that ever happened was they would circle one another,
and then move apart. Everyone knew that one time they
would finally come to blows, that sooner ro later Marvin
Macy and Miss Amelia would fight, would set upon one
another in a battle that would leave one of them brutally
beaten or dead. But everyone also knew that it was not yet
time.

One night, though, nearly three months after Marvin Macy
returned to town, there occurred an event which set the sure
course to calamity.

> *(Music out.*
> *Cafe scene back)*

MISS AMELIA

You finally movin' on.

MARVIN MACY

Yeah?

MISS AMELIA

Well, you all packed.

COUSIN LYMON
(From his throne on the barrel)

Amelia!
(Brief silence; she looks to him)
Marvin Macy is goin' to visit a spell with us.

MISS AMELIA
(After quite a pause, shakes her head as if to clear it)
I don't understand you, Cousin Lymon.

COUSIN LYMON

I said: Marvin Macy is goin' to visit a spell with us. (*Slowly, distinctly*) He is goin' to move in here. (*Pause, as nothing seems to have registered*) He is gonna live here. With us.
(*A stock-still silence, broken by*)

MISS AMELIA
(*Finally: to* MARVIN MACY)

Ain't no room.

MARVIN MACY (*Mocking*)

Ain't no room, huuh?

MISS AMELIA

This ain't no flop house . . . for convicts.

MARVIN MACY
(*His eyes still on* MISS AMELIA)

Cousin Lymon? They ain't no room for me?

COUSIN LYMON (*Imperious*)

Amelia!
(SHE *turns her sad attention to him*)
Amelia, I think I told you Marvin Macy is gonna live here with us.

MISS AMELIA
(*Surprisingly helpless before his tone*)

But . . . but, Cousin Lymon . . .

COUSIN LYMON
(*Giving orders, but taking a childish pleasure in the power of it*)

Marvin Macy will sleep in your Papa's big bed, an' we will

move what you have referred to as my coffin—my tiny bed—
into your room . . . an' you . . .
                    (HE *pauses here for full effect*)
. . . an' you, Amelia . . . well, you can pull up a mattress,
an' sleep by the stove down here.
            (*More silence, broken only by* MARVIN MACY'S *soft,
            throaty chuckle*)

                    HENRY MACY
            (*Quietly, to the bottle in front of him on the table*)
Lord God in heaven.

                    MISS AMELIA
                (*Tries to speak, but all that emerges is*)
Arrggh . . . uh, uh, arrggh.

                    COUSIN LYMON
                (*Oblivious to her attempted reply*)
So, you see, Amelia, there *is* room, after all. It merely a
question of makin' space.

                    MACPHAIL
                (*Rises, but does not move*)
I think I goin' home.

                    MRS. PETERSON
                (*Not moving at all*)
Yes; me, too.

                    SECOND TOWNSWOMAN
Think you right.

                    COUSIN LYMON
                (*Jumping off the barrel*)

So! Now I think Marvin an' I move upstairs an' get things arranged comfortable. Marvin?

MARVIN MACY
(Picking up his tin suitcase)

Comin'.

> (MISS AMELIA *has not moved; will not look at any-*
> *one.* MARVIN MACY *follows* COUSIN LYMON *up the*
> *stairs;* THEY *vanish. All the* TOWNSPEOPLE, *save* HENRY
> MACY *slowly exit now, all of them, save* MERLIE
> RYAN, *who just sort of drifts out, pausing briefly by*
> MISS AMELIA, *either to say goodnight, or touch her*
> *by the elbow, or just stop, then move on. When*
> THEY *have all left the cafe and are nearly off-stage,*
> MISS AMELIA *rouses herself slightly from her leth-*
> *argy, looks slowly around the cafe, and moves out*
> *on to the porch, where* SHE *sits, staring vacantly*
> *off.*
> *Music here, maybe a move back.*
> *The lights go down on the cafe, its interior van-*
> *ishes, and then* HENRY MACY *comes out the door*
> *and sits fairly near* MISS AMELIA)

MISS AMELIA *(After a pause)*

Henry?

HENRY MACY

Yes, Miss Amelia.

> *(All the speeches slowly responded to now)*

MISS AMELIA

I gotta do it now.

HENRY MACY

Do . . . what, Miss Amelia?

MISS AMELIA

I gotta get your brother.

HENRY MACY

Yes.

MISS AMELIA

I gotta drive him off, or kill him, or . . .

HENRY MACY

I know.

MISS AMELIA

But if I do that . . .

HENRY MACY

If you do that, what?

MISS AMELIA

If I drive him off then . . . then Cousin Lymon go off with him.

HENRY MACY

Oh, Miss Amelia . . .

MISS AMELIA

He would! I'd 'a done it long before now . . . 'cept . . .

HENRY MACY

'Cept you think Cousin Lymon go off too; go off with him?

MISS AMELIA

Unh-hunh.

HENRY MACY

But . . . but do it matter that much?

MISS AMELIA
(Looking at him finally)

Cousin Lymon go off . . . I all alone.

HENRY MACY

He ain't . . . much comfort, Cousin Lymon.

MISS AMELIA

He some. He been some. I gonna get your brother, Henry.

HENRY MACY
(Thinks; acquiesces to it)

All right. *(Pause)* Night, Miss Amelia.

MISS AMELIA

Night, Henry.

HENRY MACY
(Starting to walk off; stops, makes a statement)

Ain't nothin' I can do, is there.

MISS AMELIA
(Rising, starting to go indoors)

No. Ain't nothin', Henry.

HENRY MACY

No. Well . . . night.
(HE moves off exits)

MISS AMELIA

Night, Henry.
(SHE goes indoors)

Music up.
Lights up to daylight. Only the outside of the cafe
is seen.

THE NARRATOR
And the fight, which everybody had expected but nobody had
known exactly when it would happen, took place, when it
finally occurred, on Ground Hog's Day.
(Appropriate action for the following)
And it was at the same time both a solemn and a festive oc-
casion. Bets had been placed—with Emma Hale's money going on Marvin Macy, of course. And Miss Amelia had lay flat
down on her porch to rest her strength for the fight, and
Marvin Macy sat nearby with a tin can of hog fat between
his knees and carefully greased his arms and legs. Everybody
knew, and they did not need Cousin Lymon as their clarion
—though of course they could not stop him.

COUSIN LYMON (To MARVIN MACY)
You grease up good, now; you be real slippery she can't get a
good grip on you.

MARVIN MACY (*Greasing his arm*)
That what I doin'; don't you worry.

COUSIN LYMON
(*To some of the* TOWNSPEOPLE *who are beginning to*
saunter in)
Today! It gonna be today!

STUMPY
Yeah, we know; we know.

THIRD TOWNSMAN
Yeah, don't worry, now; we know.

COUSIN LYMON
(Beside himself with excitement, stops briefly at
MARVIN MACY)
You grease real good now.
(Darts off toward MISS AMELIA)

MARVIN MACY
(As HE *greases the other arm)*
Yeeessssss!!

COUSIN LYMON
(On his way to MISS AMELIA, *spies other* TOWNS-
PEOPLE *entering from the other side)*
The fight startin'! It about to begin.
(Moves toward MISS AMELIA *again)*

HENRY MACY *(Sadly; impatiently)*
We *know!* We know!

EMMA
An' I gonna win me a dollar today, too.

MRS. PETERSON *(Stuck-up)*
Don't see how that can be, since *I* gonna win one.

EMMA *(A gay laugh)*
You see.

COUSIN LYMON
(Now by where MISS AMELIA *is lying)*
Amelia?

MISS AMELIA
*(Not moving; staring at the sky; little expression in
her voice)*
Yes, Cousin Lymon?

COUSIN LYMON *(All excitement)*

You . . . you restin' for the fight, huuh?

MISS AMELIA

Yes, Cousin Lymon.

COUSIN LYMON

An' . . . an' . . . you eat good?

MISS AMELIA

Yes, Cousin Lymon; I had me three helpings of rare roast.

COUSIN LYMON

Marvin ate *four*.

MISS AMELIA

Good for him.

COUSIN LYMON
(A tentative finger out to touch her)

He . . . Marvin all greased up. You . . . you greased,
Amelia?

MISS AMELIA

Yes, Cousin Lymon.

COUSIN LYMON
*(Takes a step or two back, looks around the crowd,
seems to be pleading)*

Then . . . then you both about ready, I . . . I'd say.
(To STUMPY MACPHAIL*)*
I'd say they both about ready.
*(*EVERYBODY *is on stage, now, the* TOWNSPEOPLE *still
peripheral)*

MACPHAIL *(Piqued)*

I'll decide on that.

COUSIN LYMON
(Moving to one side, a curved smile on his lips)

I just tryin' to be helpful.

HENRY MACY

You be more help you go hide under a log, or somethin'.

MACPHAIL
(Moves over to MARVIN MACY*)*

You all fixed an' ready, Marvin?

MARVIN MACY
(Rises, rubs a little more grease into his arms)

Never be readier!

MACPHAIL
(Moving toward where MISS AMELIA *is lying;* SHE
sits up)

You . . . you all ready, Miss Amelia?

MISS AMELIA

I been ready for years.

MACPHAIL
(Moves front and center)

Well, then, you two c'mere.

MERLIE RYAN

What . . . what gonna happen?
*(*MISS AMELIA *and* MARVIN MACY *slowly approach
front and center)*

EMMA *(Answering* MERLIE RYAN*)*
Marvin Macy gonna kill Miss Amelia, Merlie; that what
gonna happen.

MRS. PETERSON
Other way 'round!

MERLIE RYAN
Why . . . why they gonna fight?

SECOND TOWNSMAN
Hush, you.

MERLIE RYAN *(A lonely child)*
I wanna know why. I wanna know why Marvin an' Miss
Amelia gonna kill t'other.

THIRD TOWNSMAN *(Laughing)*
'Cause they know each other, Merlie.
*(A couple of people laugh at this, but mostly there
is tense silence)*

MERLIE RYAN *(Same)*
'T'ain't no good reason.

EMMA
It gonna have to do.

MACPHAIL
(To MARVIN MACY *and* MISS AMELIA, *who come and
stand, one to either side of him.* MARVIN MACY *is
stripped to the waist, his trouser legs folded up to
above the knees;* MISS AMELIA *has her sleeves rolled
up to the tops of her shoulders, her jean legs pulled
up, too)*
Got knives, either of you?

MISS AMELIA & MARVIN MACY

Nope.

MACPHAIL

I gotta check anyway. (HE *feels into* MARVIN's *back pockets*)
You clean.

MARVIN MACY *(Vicious)*

What you think I be . . . a liar?

MACPHAIL *(Stony)*

Knives has a way of slippin' into pockets sometimes without
a person knowin' about 'em, Marvin. You musta seen a lot of
that in your time.

MARVIN MACY
(Ugly, but not about to argue further)

Yeah?

MISS AMELIA *(Impatiently)*

Come on!

MARVIN MACY
(At MISS AMELIA; *soft and wicked)*

Oh, I can't wait.

MACPHAIL *(To quiet them)*

All right! All right, now.
(Tense silence from everyone; MISS AMELIA *and* MAR-
VIN MACY *move a bit apart, stand in boxing poses,
ready)*
All right! Begin!
*(*THE FIGHT: *They circle for a moment, and then
both strike out simultaneously, without warning.
Both blows land well and stun both fighters for a
little.* THEY *circle more, then* THEY *join and mix in*

vicious in-fighting. MISS AMELIA *gets hit, staggers backwards, almost falls, rights herself.* THEY *in-fight again.* MARVIN MACY *gets struck a hard blow, staggers back.* THEY *in-fight again. Suddenly the fight shifts from boxing to wrestling. At this, the crowd comes in closer. The fighters battle muscle to muscle hipbones braced against each other; gradually* MISS AMELIA *gains the advantage, and inch by inch* SHE *bends* MARVIN MACY *over backwards, forcing him to the ground.* COUSIN LYMON *is extremely agitated. Finally,* MISS AMELIA *has* MARVIN MACY *to the ground, and straddles him, her hands on his throat. The crowd presses closer, to watch the kill)*

MRS. PETERSON *(Shrieking)*

Kill him! Kill him!

MERLIE RYAN *(Taking it up)*

Kill him! Kill him!

COUSIN LYMON
(Half a shriek, half a word, howled)
NNNNNNOOOOOOOOOOOOO!
*(*COUSIN LYMON *races from where* HE *has been standing, mounts* MISS AMELIA'S *back and begins choking her from behind)*

HENRY MACY

Stop him!

EMMA

Get her; get her!
*(*COUSIN LYMON *continues choking* MISS AMELIA, *and this is enough to shift the balance of the fight.* MARVIN MACY *manages to get* MISS AMELIA'S *hands from his throat, forces her down.* COUSIN LYMON *backs off*

a few steps. MARVIN MACY *straddles* MISS AMELIA, *beats her senseless, furiously, excessively, as the crowd gasps, yells.*
All becomes silence. Music stops. The crowd moves back a bit. MARVIN MACY *rises from the prostrate form of* MISS AMELIA; *he breathes heavily, stands over her, barely able to stand, himself)*

HENRY MACY *(Very quietly)*
Oh, Lord, no.
(All is very still, the loudest sound MARVIN MACY'S *breathing. Some of the* TOWNSPEOPLE *begin to wander dreamily off)*

EMMA
(Moving toward MISS AMELIA; *great solicitude)*
Oh, poor Miss Amelia, poor . . .

HENRY MACY
Leave her be.
*(*EMMA *obeys, exits, leaving, finally, only* MISS AMELIA, MARVIN MACY, COUSIN LYMON *and* HENRY MACY *on stage.*
MISS AMELIA *slowly pulls herself up on one arm, crawls slowly, painfully from where* SHE *has been lying to the steps, up them, collapses again on the porch.*
COUSIN LYMON *walks slowly, shyly over to* MARVIN MACY *who puts his arm around him, still breathing hard, still looking at* MISS AMELIA.
HENRY MACY *takes a few tentative steps toward* MISS AMELIA, *changes his mind, begins to exit)*

MARVIN MACY
'Bye, Henry.

HENRY MACY *(Continuing out)*
'Bye Marvin.

COUSIN LYMON
'Bye, Henry.
> (HENRY MACY *exits, as if* HE *had not heard* COUSIN
> LYMON)
>
> *(Music up)*

THE NARRATOR
> *(Tableau, with* MARVIN MACY, COUSIN LYMON *to-*
> *gether,* MISS AMELIA *sprawled on the porch)*

Marvin Macy and Cousin Lymon left town that night, but
before they went away, they did their best to wreck the store.
They took what money there was in the cafe, and the few
curios and pieces of jewelry Miss Amelia kept upstairs; and
they carved vile words on the cafe tables. After they had done
all this . . . they left town . . . together.

> (MARVIN MACY *and* COUSIN LYMON *stand for a mo-*
> *ment,* MARVIN MACY *breathing a little less hard,*
> *laughing a little)*

MARVIN MACY
(With a small chuckle)
C'mon, peanut; let's go.
> *(The two exit,* MARVIN MACY'S *arm still over* COUSIN
> LYMON'S *shoulder.* MISS AMELIA *is left alone on stage)*

> SHE *rights herself to a sitting position, howls once,*
> *becomes silent.*
> *Music continues to the end of the play.*

THE NARRATOR
And every night thereafter, for three years, Miss Amelia sat

out on the front steps, alone and silent, looking down the road and waiting. But Cousin Lymon never returned. Nothing more was ever heard of Marvin Macy or Cousin Lymon. The cafe, of course, never reopened, and life in the town was that much drearier.

(MRS. PETERSON *comes on, timidly, advances to where* MISS AMELIA *is sitting*)

And Miss Amelia closed the general store, as well, or it would be more correct to say that she discouraged anyone from coming there anymore.

MRS. PETERSON (*Quietly*)

Miss Amelia?

(MISS AMELIA *looks at her after a moment, says nothing*)

I . . . I wondered . . . I thought I would buy a coke.

MISS AMELIA
(*No expression, save some vague loss*)

Sure. (*Not moving*) That will be a dollar and five cents.

MRS. PETERSON
(*Still quiet, but flustered*)

But . . . but a coke be a nickel.

MISS AMELIA
(*Looking steadily at her; blank voice*)

Yes. (*Pause*) Five cents for the coke, and a dollar for seein' me. A dollar for lookin' at the freak.

MRS. PETERSON
(*Moving away, slowly at first, then fleeing*)

Oh . . . Miss Amelia . . .

(MISS AMELIA *alone on stage. Gets up, goes indoors, closes the door after her. Lights up to opening of the play*)

THE NARRATOR

And at the end of three years Miss Amelia went indoors one night, climbed the stairs, and never again left her upstairs rooms.

The town is dreary. On August afternoons the road is empty, white with dust, and the sky above is bright as glass. If you walk along the main street there is nothing whatsoever to do. Nothing moves—there are no children's voices, only the hum of the mill.

(The upstairs window opens and closes as in the beginning of the play, accompanying the below)

Though sometimes, in the late afternoon, when the heat is at its worst, a hand will slowly open the shutter of the window up there, and a face will look down at the town . . . a terrible, dim face . . . like the faces known in dreams. The face will linger at the window for an hour or so, then the shutters will be closed once more, and as likely as not there will not be another soul to be seen along the main street. Heat . . . and silence. There is nothing whatsoever to do. You might as well walk down to the Fork Falls Road and watch the chain gang. The twelve mortal men . . . who are together.

The Ballad of the Sad Cafe . . . the end.

(Music holds for four seconds, stops. Silence for four seconds)

CURTAIN

CARSON MCCULLERS

Mrs. McCullers was born in Columbus, Georgia. At the age of seventeen she came to New York. She studied at Columbia and New York Universities. When she was nineteen, Story magazine accepted two of her stories. Three years later her first novel The Heart is a Lonely Hunter was published by Houghton Mifflin. The year was 1940. Her published books have been Reflections in a Golden Eye (1941), The Member of the Wedding (1946), which she adapted into play form and which received the New York Drama Critics Circle Award for Best Play as well as the Donaldson Award. Her novella The Ballad of the Sad Cafe was published in 1951, her play The Square Root of Wonderful, 1957, and her novel Clock Without Hands in 1961. All of her works have been translated into more than a dozen languages.

EDWARD ALBEE

Mr. Albee was born March 12, 1928, in Washington, D.C., and began writing plays thirty years later. His plays are in order of composition, THE ZOO STORY (1958); THE DEATH OF BESSIE SMITH (1959); THE SANDBOX (1959); THE AMERICAN DREAM (1960); WHO'S AFRAID OF VIRGINIA WOOLF? (1961-1962); and THE BALLAD OF THE SAD CAFE, an adaptation of Carson McCullers' novella (1963). He is presently at work on two plays: THE SUBSTITUTE SPEAKER and TINY ALICE and a novel, which is presently titled STEP.